TAGGED

Mara Purnhagen

HARLEQUIN®
TEEN

HARLEQUIN®
TEEN

ISBN-13: 978-0-373-21007-7

TAGGED

Copyright © 2010 by Mara Purnhagen

Recycling programs for this product may not exist in your area.

For my parents, who taught me to love books

1

WHEN I GOT OFF THE BUS that crisp January morning and stepped onto the parking lot, the only thing I could see was a crowd of students gathered near the east wall of our school. It looked like some sort of outdoor rock concert, except instead of holding up lighters and swaying to a heavy guitar ballad, people were raising their cell phones to snap pictures and inching forward amid the rumbling.

I had expected the usual zombie-like trance as six hundred sleep-deprived students shuffled silently toward the back doors, carrying their withered backpacks and a deep-seated grudge at being forced to return to the narrow hallways of Cleary High School after two weeks of holiday vacation. But instead of groggy bitterness, everyone seemed filled with a strange, contagious energy. I wondered briefly if the entire student body had descended upon Something's Brewing and consumed triple-mocha espressos. Nothing else could explain the wide smiles and whooping sounds emanating from the crowd.

I scanned the crowd, searching for my best friend, Lan, but it was nearly impossible with all the people. Everyone seemed to be standing in the same small space, squeezed in between the parked cars and cedar bushes. My cell phone rang and I set my backpack down on the pavement so I could fish it out.

"Kate, where are you?" It was Lan.

"I just got here. I can't see you."

"Look toward the back doors."

I looked over and saw a hand waving from behind a cluster of ball-capped heads. "I'll be there as soon as I can."

I slowly made my way through the crowd, which wasn't easy. No one was moving. They were either talking on their phones or trying to lift each other up to see the east wall. I saw one kid try to climb on top of a car, setting off a piercing alarm.

"This better be good," I grumbled to myself. Large crowds remind me of cattle, make me feel as if I were just one of the herd. The good part, though, was that you could blend in with everyone else.

"Kate! Over here!"

I finally made it all the way to where Lan was standing. Normally, Lan stood out in any crowd. It wasn't just that she was the only Vietnamese student at Cleary High School (or in the entire town of Cleary, South Carolina, for that matter) or that she was exceptionally pretty, with long, jet-black hair that she liked to wear in a thick braid that trailed down her back. Lan possessed a sense of style that set her apart from everyone else. Even her name was interesting. It meant *orchid* in Vietnamese and, to make sure everyone knew it, Lan collected all things orchid, from the delicate jeweled pins she made herself and wore on a regular basis to the live orchids she kept in her room, each one a different color and each one occupying a small ceramic vase.

Watch for the first book in Mara Purnhagen's new series, Past Midnight

The daughter of acclaimed paranormal researchers, Charlotte Silver suddenly finds herself at the forefront of her parents' latest investigation when she's forced to solve a hundred-year-old missing persons case or learn to live with angry spirits. But it's hard to focus on the ghosts plaguing her dreams when she's adjusting to a new school and a new set of friends with ghostly secrets of their own....

On sale September 2010
Past Midnight

There was suddenly a break in the crowd and I could finally get a glimpse of what had everyone so excited. I almost smiled when I saw it. Almost. Then I glanced around for my dad. As soon as he heard about this, he'd be here, sirens wailing. I didn't see him yet, though, so I turned back to look at the wall. There, painted in thick black against the pale concrete, were half a dozen enormous gorillas.

"Isn't it amazing? Carter's going to lose it."

I agreed that, yes, Principal Carter was definitely going to lose it. This wasn't your everyday, hastily scribbled graffiti. The gorillas were absolutely lifelike, complete with shadows and stern expressions. They sat staring out at us with huge, watery eyes. Each gorilla was at least four feet tall, and the one in the middle had a thought bubble painted over its head. "So this is what the jungle looks like," it read.

Lan was exotic without trying to be, unlike me, who was just about as average as humanly possible. Brown hair, brown eyes. Even my name was average. There were times when I wished I possessed a little of Lan's uniqueness, but I'd learned that it was better not to stand out. I liked to fade into the background and watch people from a distance. Maybe that was why Lan and I were such good friends: we balanced each other out.

I gave her a quick hug. "Good to see you."

She hugged me back. "It's been forever," she agreed.

We hadn't seen each other since winter break had begun. Lan had been on vacation in Florida with her dad while I had been sprawled out in the den at home watching reality show marathons on TV and consuming way too many carbohydrates. We e-mailed and sent text messages, but I was surprised at how much I had missed my best friend.

I stood on my tiptoes in an attempt to get a view of the wall. "What are we trying to look at?"

She smiled mysteriously. "You'll see."

"There's too many people," I complained.

There was suddenly a break in the crowd and I could finally get a glimpse of what had everyone so excited. I almost smiled when I saw it. Almost. Then I glanced around for my dad. As soon as he heard about this, he'd be here, sirens wailing. I didn't see him yet, though, so I turned back to look at the wall. There, painted in thick black against the pale concrete, were half a dozen enormous gorillas.

"Isn't it amazing? Carter's going to lose it."

I agreed that yes, Principal Carter was definitely going to lose it. This wasn't your everyday, hastily scribbled graffiti. The gorillas were absolutely lifelike, complete with shadows and stern expressions. They sat staring out at us with huge, watery eyes. Each gorilla was at least four feet tall, and the one in the middle had a thought bubble painted over its head. "So this is what the jungle looks like" it read.

"This must have taken hours," I said. "Who did it?"

It was a stupid question. Everyone already knew.

Lan nodded her head toward the corner. "One guess."

I could see Trent off to one side, videotaping the crowd and smiling. He was easy to spot because he was the tallest guy at school. Trent Adams, celebrated senior and master of school pranks. He had released twenty chickens in the cafeteria during the first week of his freshman year in protest over the nuggets. As a sophomore he managed to break into the school and move every piece of the principal's office furniture outside. He re-arranged everything just as it had been inside, only now the desk and file cabinets and chairs and plants sat in the middle of the parking lot. That prank made both the local news and school legend. As a junior he decided that he would sing every word that came out of his mouth. There are very few people on this earth who can get away with singing nonstop and still be thought of as cool, but Trent managed to pull it off with ease.

A smaller group of kids had gathered around Trent. Most of them I knew, like Brady Barber and Eli James, who were hard to miss. Not only did they always hang out together, but they always dressed the same, too: baggy black pants, white collared shirt, black hoodie jacket. Reva Abbott was also standing near Trent, wearing tight clothes and a bored expression.

"What I meant to ask was, how did Trent do it?" The mural looked polished and professional. Not the work of an amateur at all. It appeared as if the gorillas had been painted using some kind of laser program—they were that perfect. In fact, it looked like it was the same gorilla copied six times, because they were identical to one another. There was no way it was done freehand, I realized. But there was also no way that Trent had access to the kind of sophisticated equipment I would guess something like this required.

"He's a genius," Lan said. "Who knows how he did it?" She stared across the crowd to watch him. Lan had always harbored a secret crush on Trent. Sometimes they flirted, but it had never developed into anything.

I reached into my backpack and pulled out the digital camera my parents had given me for Christmas. It made a sound like tinkling bells when I turned it on. I took as many shots as I could of the wall, knowing that some of the shots would be blocked by people's heads.

"We might want to get out of here now," Lan whispered. A police car had pulled into the parking lot. Two officers got out, and kids automatically walked away. One of the officers saw me, smiled and nodded. I nodded back, then let Lan pull me toward the front entrance.

There were still a few minutes before the first bell rang, but we were already in the junior hall, so we didn't have to hurry. When our new class schedules arrived just before break, Lan and I were thrilled to discover that we had first period history together. We had been best friends since freshman year and had never once had a class together, so this was a cause for celebration. Also, history was my favorite class. Mr. Gildea had a fun teaching style and with his bright brown eyes and wry smile he wasn't bad to look at, either.

"You're going to help me out, right?" Lan asked as we slid into desks in the middle of the room. She hated history. I always helped her with term papers and in return she helped me with science labs.

"This is going to be a great class," I told her. "I had Mr. Gildea last year. He's awesome."

"That's what you said about French, remember?" Lan grumbled.

"I didn't use the word *awesome*."

"No, I think you said it would be *très magnifique*. Which it was not. And I got a C."

I dug around in my backpack for a pen, automatically handing one to Lan, who always forgot to bring one to class.

"Oh, great. Look who has decided to grace us with her presence," Lan whispered. I looked up just as Tiffany Werner sailed into the room talking on her rhinestone-studded cell phone.

"It covers the wall," she was saying. "I mean, totally and completely. It will never come off, I'm sure. Well, of course. Uh-huh."

Tiffany Werner was the most spoiled girl I had ever known. She wore "Tiffany-blue," her signature color, every chance she got. Her parents named her after the famous jewelry store, and she loved to remind people of that fact, which seemed a little odd to me. I mean, if my parents had named me after a store, I wouldn't be bragging about it, no matter how fancy the store might be. She owned a genuine Tiffany diamond ring, and she considered herself a jewelry expert because of it. She wouldn't hesitate to lean over and grab someone's wrist to examine their bracelet or ring or watch, only to laugh and proclaim that it was a fake. She even did it to a teacher once. Tiffany had a way of taking over a classroom and making herself the center of attention, and I hated that.

She took a seat in the front, aware that we were all listening to her conversation. "The police are already here," she said, and I could feel a few people turn their heads in my direction. I pretended to study my blank notebook. "Trent's in the office now. They're questioning him."

This last comment caused a lot of murmuring in the classroom. The bell rang and Tiffany quickly shut her phone before Mr. Gildea walked into the room. He was one of the few teachers who wouldn't hesitate to confiscate a phone. Rumor had it that the bottom drawer of his desk was full of them, but I doubted it. Still, no one wanted to take a chance.

"Good morning," he said as he strode to the lectern. "And how are things in the jungle today?"

We all laughed a little. Mr. Gildea could be funny, probably because he was still young. He always wore khaki pants and a bright tie. This time it was green with thin orange stripes.

"Mr. Gildea, are they going to expel Trent for defacing school property?"

Everyone looked from Tiffany, who had asked the question, to Mr. Gildea, who was examining the attendance sheet.

"One moment, please, Miss Werner." He looked us over, checked his sheet and then put his pen down.

"Now, then, what was the question?"

Tiffany sighed loudly and repeated herself.

"I have no idea," he said, "but I'm sure the rumor mill will be up and running with an answer before lunch."

"They can't suspend him," said Brady Barber. He was slouched in a desk at the back of the classroom. "They have no proof."

"Oh, please," said Tiffany. "We all know it was him."

"So what if it was?" Brady was sitting up now. "I'm not saying he did it, but what if he did? It's art. You can't suspend people for expressing themselves with art."

"It's not art. It's called defacing public property, and it's a crime."

"That wall was already defaced, remember? It was streaked with tar from last year's roof repairs."

Tiffany sighed. "That was an accident, Brady. Not vandalism."

"It was still ugly."

"So are those gorillas."

Mr. Gildea held up one hand. "Sounds like we have a difference of opinion," he said, grinning. He loved a good debate. "You both present a valid point. Where is the line between art and vandalism?"

He went on to say that archaeologists had discovered graffiti in Roman ruins and that, in a way, it was one of the earliest art forms known to humans. Tiffany seemed to think that Mr. Gildea was taking Brady's side over hers.

"Art belongs in a museum, not smeared across a concrete wall," she announced. Well, this got the entire class talking, and I was glad that most people disagreed with her. I wanted to jump into the conversation, but I couldn't think of anything remotely meaningful to add. I wasn't like Tiffany, who could sum up her thoughts in one clear sentence. And I wasn't like Brady, who could always be counted on to come up with an idea no one else had thought of yet. Part of me wanted to be good at those things, but part of me knew that announcing my opinions out loud would automatically expose me to judgment, and that was something I could do without.

Mr. Gildea let the class debate the issue for a while before handing out our textbooks.

"I can see this isn't going to be resolved in one class period," he said just before the bell rang. "So we'll pick it up again tomorrow. Your assignment for tonight is simple—define art. Three hundred words."

Everyone groaned, and Tiffany snorted. "This has nothing to do with history."

Mr. Gildea smiled. "On the contrary. Art is a reflection of history. And this class owes you its thanks, Miss Werner. I wasn't planning on assigning homework today, but you brought up such a good point, I thought we should build on it."

Most of the class turned to glare at Tiffany while I smirked and Lan gave me a friendly nudge. If Tiffany thought she was going to run Mr. Gildea's class, she had another think coming.

The bell rang and I gathered up my things. As I was walking down the aisle, I tripped over Tiffany's foot and stumbled a little.

"Watch it," she snarled, glaring at me.

"Sorry," I mumbled, then immediately felt stupid. Why was I apologizing to her? She was the one sitting with her leg stretched across the aisle.

The rest of the day was pretty much the same. Everyone was talking about the gorillas on the wall. Trent wasn't seen at lunch, and everyone assumed he had been suspended.

"This is really odd," Lan said as we stood at our lockers at the end of the day. "No one knows what's going on. No one."

I put on my jacket. "I'll find out and let you know."

"You going to ask your dad?"

"Even better," I said. "I'll ask Trent."

I WORKED INSIDE A PURPLE triangle. It was probably the only building in the entire state of South Carolina that was shaped like a slice of pie and painted the color of a grape popsicle. It was a little coffee drive-through place called Something's Brewing. I loved it because the hours were good, the coffee was great and, best of all, there were no crowds. Something's Brewing was designed to fit two employees, a wall of coffee machines, a tiny storeroom and an even tinier bathroom in the back. Cars pulled up, people placed their orders, we handed them coffee in insulated paper cups, and they drove away, happy and fully caffeinated. Best job ever. Plus, I got free coffee, which I always seemed to need right after school.

Some days I worked with Bonnie, my boss. She was a grandmother who was supposed to retire years earlier, but opened Something's Brewing instead. "I just couldn't stay retired, you know? It got boring," she said to me once as she knitted a green sweater. I loved Bonnie. She was really easy to work with and was always in a good mood.

Most days, though, I worked with Eli James, another junior from my school and one of Trent Adams's very best friends.

Trent usually gave Eli a ride, which I was hoping would be the case that day so I could find out what was going on. Lan was counting on me. She loved knowing things other people did not, and this was the biggest scandal our school had seen since Trent filled the teachers' lounge with Styrofoam peanuts the year before.

When I arrived at Something's Brewing, Bonnie was there, wiping down the counter. "Hello, dear," she said. "What can I make you?"

She didn't really need to ask. Bonnie always made me a caramel latte. She put in just the right amount of caramel—they were perfect.

"The usual," I said, and Bonnie began to steam milk. "I thought Eli was working today."

"He is. Just running a little late, I guess."

That was interesting. Eli was never late. What if they had suspended Trent and Eli couldn't get a ride? I wanted to call Lan immediately, but a car pulled up and I had to take the order. While I was doing that, another car pulled alongside the building. I heard a door shut, and the next moment Eli walked through the back, running a hand through his chestnut-colored hair and apologizing to Bonnie for being late.

"Not a problem, dear." Bonnie treated us more like her grandchildren than her employees. She even knitted scarves for Eli and me—her "two favorite workers"—and gave them to us as Christmas gifts. She once spent a month trying to teach me how to knit, but I didn't have the patience for it. I managed to make half a scarf, although it looked more like a very fluffy dishrag. I was disappointed, but Bonnie said that not everyone had a knack for knitting.

"It's not your talent, dear," she'd said. "But don't worry, you're good at so many things."

I wanted to ask her to name some of those things I was supposedly so good at because, honestly, I didn't know. I had tried to knit because I thought it could be a retro kind of hobby, something I could be really creative with. I envisioned myself making funky sweaters and bright hats for Lan, who always made me pieces of jewelry for Christmas. The most imaginative thing I'd made for her was a CD of our favorite songs.

I placed lids on three double espressos and handed them to my customer while Bonnie gave Eli the inventory list. "I need you to check this," she said. "Especially the small cups. I don't think they sent us enough this time."

Bonnie gathered up her purse and coat, told us to have a great day and left. As soon as I saw her car pull away, I turned to Eli.

"So?"

He gave me an innocent, surprised look. "What?"

"You know exactly what," I said. "What's going on?"

He plopped down in one of the two little chairs Bonnie had set up for us. "I need a strong drink, Katie."

Eli knew I hated being called Katie. People always assumed that my name was short for Katherine, but it wasn't. My parents had named me Kate. Just Kate, pure and simple. They said they didn't want anything fancy or something that could be turned into a nickname, which was fine by me. Still, sometimes I wished I had a more sophisticated name, like Isabelle or Olivia.

I glared at Eli. "If I make you a drink, will you tell me everything you know?"

"Depends on how good the drink is."

I turned to the coffee machine. I always made Eli a special drink, something not on the menu. It was a latte, but extra strong. I added shots of chocolate and caramel, and just a hint of praline. Eli said it tasted like a candy bar. He called it a "Katie Bar" for a while until I threatened to stop making them. No one calls me Katie, I don't care how cute they are.

I made his drink and handed it to him.

"I hope you didn't skimp on the chocolate," he said.

"Would you like to drink it or wear it?" I asked him sweetly. He smiled and took a sip.

"Perfect," he announced. "So, what was it you wanted to know?"

I sat down across from him, which was kind of hard to do. Eli was tall and lanky, and his knees bumped into my legs. "I want to know everything," I said. "What happened to Trent? Where is he? Why were you late to work?"

Eli smiled and took an extra-slow sip. He was torturing me and enjoying every second of it.

"Trent is alive and well," he said finally. "He is at home. I was late because Brady's new girlfriend is incredibly slow and we couldn't leave without her." He wrinkled his nose. "I mean, we could have and maybe we should have because she's really annoying, if you ask me."

"I didn't ask you about Brady's girlfriend. I asked about Trent. Is he suspended? Did they take him to the police station?"

Eli raised an eyebrow at me. "I thought you would know that."

"Just because my dad's the police chief doesn't mean he tells me everything. In fact, I probably know less than anyone else about what goes on in this town."

Dad tended to keep things to himself, which I appreciated. Occasionally, he would relate some police-related story at dinner, but only if it was funny—like a naked guy stuck in a tree, which happened a lot more than you would think—or strange—snakes discovered in a car, for example. Everyone seemed to think that I did know things or, worse, that I was potentially a rat. Sometimes kids would stop talking if I was close by. But my dad and I had an understanding that I would go to him if, and only if, someone was in danger of hurting themselves or someone else. Other than that, I was not responsible for the actions of others. Of course, try telling that to the entire school. Any time a party got busted, people looked at me funny the next day, like I was somehow responsible. Lan thought I was imagining things, but I knew I wasn't. My dad's job created a negative side effect for me: it made me stand out during those times when I most wanted to fade away.

"I don't know anything," I repeated.

Eli pulled his laptop out of his backpack. "I believe you," he said. "Unfortunately, I don't know anything, either." He began typing.

"You must know something," I protested. "You're his best friend."

Eli didn't answer me. He was staring at his computer screen. "Just checking my e-mail," he said softly. I could tell he was reading, and once Eli got into his computer, forget it. He completely focused on that and nothing else. "Well, Trent's not suspended," he said finally. "Yet."

A car pulled up to the window and Eli stood up. It was a big order: five drinks, each one different, including a strawberry cheesecake cappuccino, which is a hassle to make. Eli started on a low-fat, almond latte while I handled the cash register. We worked well together. Eli was fast and efficient, and I double-checked everything, made sure the lids were on tight and cleaned up afterward. After our customer left, Eli sat back down at his computer while I rinsed out the steamer cups.

"So he e-mailed you?" I asked.

"Yeah, but it's brief." Eli read aloud from the message Trent had sent: "I'll be back at school tomorrow. They're checking my alibi. Not to worry, it's all good. No proof, no crime." Eli started to say something else, but stopped. I knew he was holding back, but I wasn't going to push it.

"I wonder what his alibi is."

Eli yawned. "He was out of town visiting relatives."

"So you do know more than you're telling me."

He smiled and shook his head. "Why does everyone assume it was someone from our school?"

"Who else would do that to the building?" I wiped the counter and made sure we had enough medium-sized cups. I knew we'd be getting an after-work rush in a half hour, and nearly everyone ordered a medium.

I glanced at Eli, who was still typing away at his computer. I wanted to remind him to do the inventory, but I also knew he would get it done and I didn't want to sound like a nag. If Eli was anything, it was reliable. And adorable, in a way. When we first began working together over the summer, I thought he was potential boyfriend material, but the timing was off. He had just started dating Reva, a junior who came around all the time to gaze at him and glare at me, and I was just breaking up with Kevin Cleaver, a senior I had dated for a total of three months.

Kevin and I had dated casually because we both knew he was leaving for college at the end of the summer. He took me to the prom, where we danced and laughed and ate chicken Marsala. We had fun, and I thought we would keep seeing each other until August, when he left for school.

Then, a month before he was supposed to leave, he announced that he'd been "hooking up" with a college girl he met at a party. It was the first time anyone had broken up with me. Kevin just stood there, his hands shoved into his pockets, and shrugged. "We both knew this wasn't a long-term thing, right?" he asked, and I nodded and said something like "Yeah, sure, no big deal." But I was crushed. It actually surprised me that I was so hurt. I mean, I knew it was a temporary thing, but still. I guess it was the fact that I had been so easily replaced. I thought I had mattered to him at least a little, and when I realized I hadn't, I felt even worse.

"You look tired," I said to Eli. He had dark circles beneath his eyes and he kept yawning.

"I need to get back on schedule," he said, not taking his eyes off the computer. "I stayed up too late over break. Ben was in town and he never sleeps."

Eli's brother Ben went to college out West somewhere, where he was an undeclared senior. According to Eli, Ben changed his major every semester and would be in school at least another three years.

Eli looked at me. "So, what did you think of it?"

"Think of what?" I was debating whether or not to bring

another bottle of almond syrup out of the back room. We were getting low.

"The gorillas. What did you think of the gorillas?"

"I think someone wasted an awful lot of time and effort. I mean, they're just going to be removed."

"But what did you think about the actual gorillas? Did you like them? Hate them? Anything?"

I considered it. My first thought had been that someone— most likely Trent—was going to be in a lot of trouble. But I also thought that the gorillas had been very well done. Beautiful, almost.

Eli would probably think I was crazy if I called them beautiful, so instead I said, "We debated it in history. You know, whether it was art or just vandalism."

"And?" Eli seemed pretty intent on the topic.

"And the class was fairly divided."

"Which side were you on?"

I knew what he wanted me to say. Despite his claims that he didn't know anything, Eli was almost certainly covering for Trent.

"I haven't decided," I said finally.

Eli stood up and stretched. "Well, let me know when you do," he said. "I'm going to do the inventory. If you get a chance, check out the article on my computer."

After he went back to the storage room, I sat down and picked up the laptop. The screen showed the front page of a newspaper from Tennessee. Mt. Juliet Encounters Gorilla it read. It was about a town near Nashville where a four-foot high gorilla had been painted onto the wall of an abandoned building. There was a small black-and-white picture of the building. I pulled out my camera and compared the pictures I had taken earlier in the morning to the one in the article. The gorilla was exactly the same as the ones on our school. Exactly. I checked the date of the article.

"Two days ago," I murmured. Mt. Juliet was at least a four-hour drive from Cleary, maybe more. Was that where Trent's relatives lived? If so, it was a bad alibi. And why paint the same picture in both towns? The police would be able to connect him to both places and he'd really be in trouble. If Trent's relatives did live in Mt. Juliet, it wouldn't make any sense that Eli would want me to read the article. He would be pointing the finger at his best friend. I was confused.

Eli came back from the stockroom just as cars began lining up for the after-work rush. I wasn't sure what to say to him, but fortunately we were so busy making drinks that neither one of us had time to talk. Finally, just before six, we began to close up for the day.

"So what did you think of the article?" Eli asked.

"Well, it's obviously the same guy," I said, handing him my camera. He clicked through the images I'd taken that morning.

"These are good," he said. He paused at a shot I'd taken of the crowd. "This one's really good."

I looked over his shoulder. The picture on the screen showed one of my crowd shots. A group of freshmen boys had just moved in front of me, blocking my view of the wall. One of the boys was holding something in his cupped hands, and the others looked down at what he held, smiling. I didn't get a look at what was in the boy's hands, and just after I took the picture, they walked away.

"The gorillas aren't even in that one," I pointed out.

"I know, but it's still a good shot. Very clear. Plus, it's not staged. There's something real there."

"I guess."

Eli turned off the camera and handed it back to me. "You should take more pictures like that."

"I think people would notice if I stood around taking pictures of them."

"Maybe. Maybe not. You could try to, you know, stay out of the way."

Something I tried to do every day, I thought. But taking pictures of unsuspecting students seemed like an odd thing to do if you weren't on the yearbook staff.

"Think about it," Eli said.

"Um, okay."

I wasn't sure what else I was supposed to say. Eli and I cleaned up and locked the doors. Brady was waiting for him in the parking lot. He waved at me. "Hey, Kate!"

I could see Reva in the backseat of Brady's car. She looked at me, scowled and then smiled wide when Eli opened the door. Eli turned to me just before getting in the car. "You okay with a ride?"

"My dad's coming," I said.

"We'd better get out of here, then. Brady's tags are expired." He smiled so I would know he was joking and got in the backseat next to Reva. I watched them leave, still trying to figure out not only why Eli had shown me the article possibly connecting Trent to two separate acts of vandalism, but why he had seemed so intense about me taking more pictures. Did he think I was actually good at it, or was he just trying to get me off the topic of the gorillas?

Minutes later, Dad pulled his police cruiser into the parking lot and I got into the front seat.

"How was your day?" he asked.

"It was very strange," I replied.

LAN WAS MORE THAN A LITTLE disappointed that I didn't have any real news about Trent. "But he's definitely coming to school tomorrow?" she asked for the tenth time.

"Definitely," I assured her. I was talking to her on my cell phone while I searched the Internet for "gorilla graffiti," in the upstairs office. My parents wouldn't let me have a computer in my room. They said anything I needed to search for could be done in public, which was just their way of saying that they didn't want me looking at naked people online.

I wanted to read through the Tennessee newspaper article again. I felt like I was missing something. Lan moved off the topic of Trent and on to Mr. Gildea's class.

"No one else assigned a paper on the first day back," she complained. "What am I supposed to write?"

"It sounds fairly easy, Lan. Just do a Web search. You can write three hundred words about art in ten minutes."

"No, *you* can write three hundred words in ten minutes. It'll take me hours."

Mom called me downstairs for dinner and I told Lan I had to go.

"By the way, did you hear about Tiffany's party?" she asked before I could hang up.

"She's always having a party." Every time her parents took a weekend "holiday," Tiffany threw some kind of wild celebration for half the school.

"This is different. It's her birthday party, and apparently she's going all out. As in, bigger than homecoming and prom put together."

"Well, I'm sure it will be lovely. Gotta go."

I had never been invited to one of Tiffany's parties, and I didn't think she was going to start putting me on the guest list now. I guessed it would be nice to see what all the fuss was about, but at the same time, I knew I'd feel completely out of place with Tiffany's crowd.

My parents were already sitting at the dining-room table when I walked in.

"How's Lan?" Mom asked as she scooped steaming vegetables onto her plate.

I took my seat and dug into a bowl of pasta salad. "Good. She's freaking out about a history paper we have due tomorrow."

"A paper on the first day back? Good," Dad said. He approved of hard work, strict teachers and rigid rules. Dinner, for example, was nonnegotiable in our house. We ate dinner together six days a week, with only Friday as an exception. My parents kept strange hours and dinner was the one time we were all together.

Sometimes Dad was called out in the middle of the night, and Mom worked at Cleary Confections, the local bakery, and usually got up around four in the morning, which I considered inhumane. Mom was in charge of cakes. Birthday, wedding, graduation—she made them all, from plain yellow with chocolate frosting to a six-tiered red velvet monstrosity decorated to look like a volcano. She said baking was her "creative outlet," and she loved it. She came home smelling like buttercream icing and devising new ways to shape gum paste into flowers.

"I heard you had an exciting morning at school," Mom commented. I wasn't sure if she was talking to Dad or to me.

"You mean the graffiti? It wasn't that big a deal."

Dad looked at me. "Not a big deal? Do you have any idea how much money it's going to cost to sandblast that stuff off the wall?" He shook his head. "No one respects public property anymore."

"It was on the news at lunchtime," Mom said. "It's certainly interesting. Not your typical graffiti. It seemed more, I don't know, professional?" She looked at Dad like he might be able to supply the appropriate word.

"Well, it just might be," he admitted. He told us that Trent's alibi was a good one, that he was out of state visiting his grandmother that day. He got home around eleven, a fact established by a gas receipt, and went to bed at midnight, which was confirmed by his parents.

"And we think the vandalism occurred around 1:00 a.m.," Dad said. "He could've left after they thought he went to bed, but his folks let us search his car, and we didn't find anything. No paint, nothing. So Trent may be innocent."

Unless his parents were covering for him, I thought. Why would he be visiting his grandmother in another state the night before school began? I didn't say anything about the article I'd read, but I didn't have to. Dad had seen it, as well.

"This same thing happened in Tennessee just a few days ago. We think it was some guy traveling through town, looking to stir up a little trouble."

Mom reached for her glass of wine. "Well, it certainly is strange."

Dad shrugged. "It's probably a one-time thing. This guy tagged the town and moved on. Some other town will get those gorillas next."

"Tagged?" Mom asked.

"It's what they call it now."

After dinner I went to my room to work on my history paper. I had looked up some definitions of art and tried to find a clever way to use them. The problem, I discovered, was that no one could come up with one single definition for art. It didn't have to be beautiful if it was considered "significant." But who decided what was significant?

I figured I could spend hours on the question and still not come up with an answer, so I decided to use a quote from Hippocrates because I knew Mr. Gildea liked the Greeks. *"Vita brevis, ars longa,"* I typed at the top of the page. Then I included the translation: "Life is short, art endures." I argued that the gorillas on the school wall weren't really art because, in the end, they would not endure. They would be removed within the month, and if they had truly been art, wouldn't someone want to keep them around longer? I knew it wasn't the most solid argument, but I figured the ancient Greek quote would earn me some points and besides, weren't all teachers supposed to be opposed to defacing school property? Mr. Gildea would like it, I was sure.

I put away my schoolwork and got ready for bed. I couldn't stop thinking about the wall. I was sure Trent was behind it, but maybe someone was helping him. Maybe Brady and Reva were working with Trent, not just covering for him, but painting, as well. I told myself to stop coming up with conspiracy theories and get some sleep, but I couldn't seem to turn off my brain. As I was drifting off, another thought occurred to me: what if Eli was helping Trent?

Dᴀᴅ ᴡᴀs ᴏɴʟʏ ᴘᴀʀᴛʟʏ ʀɪɢʜᴛ about the graffiti leaving town. The gorillas did appear in another state, on the side of an abandoned restaurant in Beulah, Arkansas, a small town east of Little Rock. This time, two gorillas were pictured, and the thought bubble above their heads read "We love vegetarians." It appeared three days after our school had been "decorated." Suddenly it did not seem possible that Trent had been involved. There was just no way to drive all the way to Arkansas Wednesday after school, paint a building and be back in time for class on Thursday morning, which was exactly where Trent was.

Dad knew about it, and an online search for "gorilla graffiti" would lead someone to several articles, but most people didn't know or didn't care. Trent seemed happy enough to take credit for the prank at our school, and everyone seemed happy enough to give it to him. His adoring league of freshmen followers quickly squashed any rumors that he *wasn't* responsible for the popular artwork. Still, something felt off to me, although I wasn't sure what it was. I guess part of me hoped that Cleary did have a resident graffiti artist. The mural had caused a commotion and shattered our boring routine, if only for a little while.

On Friday, the gorilla mural at school changed. Someone had added to it. "This is art" was stenciled in the right-hand corner of the wall. One of the gorillas was now holding a paintbrush while another grasped a spray-paint can. Again, it looked professional. And again, it caused an uproar.

"It's just stupid," Tiffany Werner proclaimed during our first period debate. "I mean, they're going to sandblast it this weekend, right? So what's the point of adding to it? It's a desperate cry for attention."

I was reminded of the quote I had used in my paper defining art. I had written that it wasn't art if it did not endure. At the time, I'd believed it. I mean, all truly great art had endured, right? How old was the *Mona Lisa?*

Lan raised her hand, and Mr. Gildea nodded at her. "If he wants attention, then why has the artist remained anonymous?" she asked. "What if he doesn't want anything but for us to look at it, to enjoy it? Isn't that what art is for?"

I knew Lan was just disagreeing with Tiffany for the sake of disagreeing with her. Lan had come to school on Tuesday wearing her favorite orchid pin, the one made with hundreds of little stones in different shades of ivory and red. Tiffany noticed it and stopped in front of Lan's desk before class began.

"Are those *real* rubies?" she demanded in front of everyone.

"Of course," Lan said, making sure to look Tiffany directly in the eye.

Tiffany just smirked. "I'll bet," she said before walking away. Lan was furious and since then had been looking for any reason at all to make Tiffany look bad in public. So far, she had achieved only minor success.

Brady Barber agreed with Lan's opinion about the graffiti artist, and the debate was soon picking up speed—and volume. Mr. Gildea finally had to quiet everyone down and tell us to open our books. We were already behind, he said, but we could debate for ten minutes every morning as long as we remained civil with one another.

"Debate is probably the best learning experience you'll ever have," he said. "Second best, of course, will be learning about the Carthaginians. Turn to page sixteen."

I was relieved to finally get off the topic of the school gorillas. It was getting a little crazy. The local paper had featured a picture of the mural on its front page, and of course our student newspaper dedicated two whole pages to it, interviewing nearly everyone. I'd heard that some kids were planning to protest the sandblasting, scheduled for Saturday, but figured it was just another one of Trent's crazy ideas. He had a real knack for self-promotion.

I was still thinking about it when I arrived at work. I was expecting to find Bonnie, but Eli was there, working on his math homework.

"Bonnie's not here?" I asked.

"Don't worry, she left you something," he said.

A tall cup of caramel latte sat on the counter. I smiled and took a sip. "You know, I have these five days a week, and I'm telling you, they just keep getting better."

"You keep drinking those and you're going to become a caramel latte," Eli muttered. He was furiously erasing a prob-

lem in his notebook. I was about to offer him some help when
I heard the toilet flush.

"I thought you said Bonnie left?"

"She did."

The bathroom door opened and Reva Abbott sauntered
out. There were two things I always noticed about Reva: her
heels and her nails. She wore tall, spiky heels that made a sharp
clipping sound against the floor. I tried wearing high heels to
school once, but my feet were killing me before the end of
second period. I didn't know how Reva did it. Also, she had
the longest nails I'd ever seen on a girl. They were like talons,
and she painted them in bright, unusual colors like turquoise
or orange. That day they were deep purple, like an eggplant.

Reva stopped when she saw me, gave me a thin smile and
turned to Eli.

"I'm leaving," she said. Eli barely looked up from his work.
Reva bent down and whispered something into his ear, her
dark nails tickling the back of his neck. I turned away, flus-
tered by the intimacy of it.

I stared out the window, watching cars and warming my
hands around the steaming cup of latte. When a blue SUV
sped past, I immediately thought of Kevin. He had driven a
similar car. After prom we had spent some time in the backseat.
Nothing too heavy, just a little making out while Black
Sabbath played in the CD player. Kevin was really into classic
rock.

"Sorry about that."

I was pulled from my thoughts by Eli. When I turned
around, I was surprised to see that Reva was gone. I hadn't
heard her leave.

"Oh, no problem."

"She gave me a ride," Eli explained.

"Right. You don't have a car."

I didn't have a car, either, mainly because of my dad. He said he'd seen too much to let a teenager behind the wheel. "When you're eighteen, we'll talk," he'd promised. When I complained to Mom that it was completely unfair, she sided with Dad. "We just need to know that you can be responsible," she said, which was infuriating, because when had I ever *not* been responsible? I did well in school, went to work and came home every night for dinner. Most parents would consider me their dream child. My parents saw me as one tenuous step away from a tragic life of wild teenage debauchery.

"This summer," Eli said. "That is, my parents said they'd get me a car if I pass math." He ripped a page from his notebook and wadded it into a sharp ball. "So maybe I won't be getting a car," he said with a bitter laugh.

"What are you working on?"

"Precalculus."

"You are so lucky you know me," I joked as I sat down next to him. "Because I just happen to be a precalc *expert*."

"Lucky me," Eli agreed, although he sounded less than enthusiastic. A car pulled up to the window and Eli automatically got up while I read over his book. After he had finished with the order, Eli slumped into the chair and sighed. "It's no use," he informed me. "I can't learn this stuff. Trust me. My brain cannot process numbers."

I wondered if Eli's dark mood was due more to Reva's brief visit than from problems with precalculus. I sensed there were problems between them. Eli always seemed to pull away from her, to be uncomfortable with her, in a way. Or maybe he was just embarrassed by public displays of affection. He was one of those guys, I thought, that liked to stay in the background, someone who didn't like or need the glow of the spotlight.

Reva, on the other hand, was more outspoken. She wore heavy red lipstick and always smelled faintly of cigarette smoke. On the rare occasions I had heard her laugh, she was loud. I got the impression that she wanted people to look in her direction and see her with one arm draped across Eli.

I wasn't sure why Reva disliked me, but Lan had a theory. "She's the possessive type. She's suspicious of any girl within a mile of him, and you work next to him every day."

"So? It doesn't mean I want to date him," I argued.

"Doesn't matter," Lan had replied. "You're a threat."

It was laughable to me that anyone would see me as a threat, but I knew Lan had a point. I thought about this as I leaned over to help Eli with a calculus problem. He smelled very clean, like soap and mint mouthwash. I suddenly felt self-conscious and hoped that I smelled okay, too.

We went through Eli's assignment slowly, getting up every few minutes to serve a customer. Eli struggled with some of the problems, and I tried to break it down for him as best I could. I was very aware of his breathing, which made it difficult for me to concentrate. At one point, I realized that we were breathing in rhythm with one another, and it was all I could think about.

It took us about an hour to get through his homework, but he seemed a little more positive once we finished.

"Thanks," he said as he put away his book. "That helped. Maybe I can pass this class."

"Of course you can," I said, then felt immediately stupid. I hoped I didn't sound like his mother.

A car pulled up, its bass pumping so hard that the windows rattled.

"You guys sell burgers?" someone yelled. I was about to snap that no, we certainly did not sell fast food when Eli leaned out the window to slap hands with the driver. It was Trent Adams. Eli told him to come on in, so Trent parked his car and came around to the back.

If you saw Trent walking down the street you might assume that he played basketball. He was long and skinny and kept his dark blond hair buzzed. I could see why Lan, like half the girls at our school, found him so attractive.

"Hey, Kate," Trent said. He looked around for a place to sit, decided that the room was too small and leaned against the wall instead.

"Hi, Trent. You want something to drink?"

"Kate makes an awesome latte," Eli said.

Trent shook his head. "No. Thanks, though." He looked at Eli. "You ready for tonight?"

Eli stiffened. I thought I saw him tilt his head toward me. Trent glanced in my direction. "So, Kate," he said, switching topics completely. "Brady tells me your history class has gotten kind of interesting."

My very first thought was that he was referring to our unit on the Carthaginians and was making a joke. Then I realized that he meant the morning debates.

"Yeah, it's kind of a Tiffany versus Brady type thing," I said.

"I heard Lan was taking on Her Majesty, as well."

I knew Lan would be thrilled when I talked to her later on

and told her that Trent had actually mentioned her in conversation. I smiled. "Lan takes on a lot of things," I said. We laughed, even though I wasn't quite sure what I'd said that was so funny. I felt a little uncomfortable around Trent, like I had to try and impress him. I wanted him to think I was okay, but I didn't know why I needed his approval.

"Hey, Kate, we'll lock up tonight, okay?" Eli's back was to me as he stacked cups that didn't really need stacking.

"Oh. Okay, sure." I was confused. Eli seemed suddenly cold. He wasn't looking at me and I wondered if I'd said something to upset him.

"Nice seein' you, Kate," Trent said.

I took this as my cue to leave and gathered up my bag and pulled on my jacket. I left without saying goodbye to Eli and waited outside for my dad to arrive. I didn't have to wait long, but the entire time all I could think of was how I had been kicked out of the one place where I always felt I belonged.

EDEN ALDER WAS HAVING a heart attack. At least, that's what she told us on Monday at lunch. As editor of the *Cleary Chronicle,* our school newspaper, Eden had a "gut-wrenching" decision to make about the front page of the next issue: should she give lead-article status to the late-night protest over the "school mural" (as it was now being called) or Tiffany Werner's birthday party?

The choice seemed simple to me, but Eden was in full-out panic mode. She had three hours until deadline and her staff was in an uproar. Half wanted the protest to be featured front and center while the other half argued that it was old news and had already been covered in the local papers. Tiffany's party, however, was fresh news and of much more interest to the average Cleary High School student.

Lan and I listened to Eden as we ate our lunches. I, for one, was glad to be discussing something other than Trent Adams. I had spent the weekend at Lan's house, and all she wanted to talk about was her current crush.

"How did his voice sound when he said my name?" she asked as she made banana spring rolls. Ever since the ninth grade Lan had made it her mission in life to get me to try new foods. At her insistence, I had sampled sweet mung bean soup and carp cooked in coconut milk and thang long fish cakes. If it were up to me, I'd live on peanut butter and jelly sandwiches, but I appreciated Lan's efforts to expand my culinary horizons. Every once in a while, she made something that I loved, but most of the time I couldn't figure out what animal I was eating and wasn't sure I really wanted to know.

"His voice? It sounded the way it always sounds," I had replied.

Lan looked like she was concentrating hard on a complex chemical equation. "I need more information," she said. "Help me out here."

In the end, I retold the story of Trent's brief visit to Something's Brewing about a hundred times, never altering a detail. I didn't talk about how it made me feel to have Eli give me the cold shoulder. Lan wasn't really interested in that, anyway. She wanted to talk about Trent again at school that morning, and of course rehash it at lunch, but Eden's dilemma had taken center stage, much to my relief.

Eden sat with her head in her hands, moaning about the tough decisions she was forced to make while Lan and I tried to offer our sympathy.

"I mean, it's only the most important decision of my *life!*" Eden wailed. I glanced at Lan, who was picking at a salad. Eden had a tendency to exaggerate—not exactly a good quality in a journalist.

"I think it's pretty clear," I said. "The protest is much more interesting. It affected more students directly."

"But that's just it," Eden said. "Only three boys were arrested, and they were released with a warning two hours later. No big deal. But the party? That affects *hundreds* of students."

Tiffany Werner had announced on Friday that she was, indeed, throwing a party.

A big party.

To quote Tiffany exactly, "The biggest party this town has ever seen." Her parents had rented out the country club, hired a band and booked caterers to celebrate Tiffany's sixteenth birthday, which was, for some reason, a huge event. Monumental, people said. As if girls didn't turn sixteen every day of the year and therefore it was a rare milestone that required a celebration ten times bigger than most people's weddings.

There were a few people on the *Cleary Chronicle* staff who argued that Tiffany's party would cause issues to fly off the shelves, or in the case of the *Cleary Chronicle,* to be plucked off the tables set up outside the cafeteria.

Tiffany's story held a hint of mystery: two hundred and fifty students would be invited, but no one had yet received an invitation. The protest story had a bit of violence: a few kids had thrown bottles and were escorted "downtown," where they had to wait in a holding cell until their parents came to pick them up. My dad had been there, cuffing freshmen and putting them in the backseat of his car. I didn't ask for specifics and he didn't offer any, but it was all over school and people were giving me some distance when I walked down the hallways as if I had something to do with it.

"But, Eden," I argued, "you're always saying that the school paper is like a time capsule. When people look back on this issue in ten years, what do you think they'll find more important? A student protest or a birthday party?"

"The protest," Lan said. She knew there was no way she was getting an invitation to Tiffany's party, and I think she wanted to diminish its social importance as much as possible.

Eden seemed to consider this. She pushed her disheveled hair off her face and sat up straighter. "Okay," she said, taking a deep, dramatic breath. "You're right. Okay. I know what I have to do."

Austin McDaniel, Eden's assistant editor, came running up to our table a moment later. He plopped down in the chair next to her, out of breath. "Never. Believe. What. Happened," he gasped, his face red.

Eden went pale. "No. Austin, I absolutely cannot handle anything else right now."

Austin shook his head. "Huge. News."

Lan passed her bottled water down the table. "Here. Calm down."

Austin took a long drink. "Tiffany's party," he said as his breathing returned to normal. "It has to go on the front page."

Eden sighed. "And why is that?"

Austin smiled. "Because it's going to be on TV."

THE SCHOOL WAS IN A KIND of pandemonium. The biggest party of the year was going to be taped for an MTV special.

Anyone who had felt even a mild interest in attending was now foaming at the mouth, desperate for one of the exclusive invitations. Rumors flared up: no freshmen would be invited, all guests would be required to wear special wristbands, Tiffany's parents were spending hundreds of thousands of dollars. For her part, Tiffany stayed quiet, simply smiling demurely and twirling her hair whenever anyone asked her about it.

Of course, the party was featured on the front page of Wednesday's issue of the *Cleary Chronicle* while the student protest was demoted to the bottom corner. I was reading the protest article at Something's Brewing when Eli showed up for work. I didn't hear him enter at first, but then he cleared his throat and I looked up, startled.

"Sorry. Did you say something?" I asked. Eli had called in sick on Friday, so I spent my shift with Bonnie, who was trying to convince me to give crocheting a try. I already knew from my failed attempt at knitting that I was all thumbs with a pair of fat needles and a ball of yarn. I tried, but I couldn't get the hang of it.

"I was wondering if you could make me a drink?"

"Sure, just give me a minute."

I had read the article three times already, but I wanted to read it again.

"It says here that the protest was 'mildly successful,'" I read aloud. "What does that mean, exactly?"

I gave the paper to Eli and turned to the espresso machine so I could make him my patented Katie Bar Latte. I wanted to pretend that nothing unusual had happened the previous Thursday, that he had not hurt my feelings in any way when he asked me to leave.

"It says that the protesters were able to delay removal of the mural. I guess that's successful."

"Mildly successful," I said as I steamed the milk.

"Of course, if they were trying to make headlines, they were very unsuccessful," Eli commented. "This party has everyone going mental."

I stirred three kinds of syrup into Eli's latte. "Personally, I would have liked more information about the gorillas."

"Yeah? Like what?"

I handed Eli his drink. "Like, did they ever catch this guy? Has he struck again? Why gorillas? What's the whole point?" I had searched online to find the answers myself, but since the last gorilla had been spotted in Beulah a week earlier, there hadn't been anything new.

"Sounds like you're heading up an investigation," Eli joked. "Are you helping out your dad or something?"

"I do not work for my dad!" I shouted.

Eli looked at me like I'd just slapped him, which I suddenly had the urge to do.

"Sorry," I said, lowering my voice. "It's just that people seem to think that I snitch, which I don't."

"Okay," said Eli.

I didn't feel like he really believed me. "My dad and I have a deal—he doesn't ask and I don't tell."

"I get it."

I was embarrassed. Eli hadn't done anything intentionally cruel, and here I was, going off on him as if he'd insulted my family.

"I'm sorry for snapping at you," I said finally. "My dad's job is kind of a sore spot with me."

Eli smiled. "It's okay, really. I understand. It's my fault for making a bad joke."

A minivan pulled up to the window. The driver was a haggard-looking woman and the backseat was full of shrieking kids. "Do you have anything non-caffeinated?" she asked wearily. Eli was already pulling fruit juice out of the fridge as I typed in the order. We prepared five cups of apple juice for the kids and a double espresso for the mom in record time and handed the woman her drinks along with a full stack of napkins.

"Looks like she's having a rough day," Eli commented. I could tell he was trying to lighten the mood and change the subject, and I decided to let him. "So, we were talking about the gorillas, right?"

I smiled. "Sure."

"And you were about to tell me what you really thought of them."

"Was I?" It was flattering, I thought, that Eli seemed to really want to know my opinion. The truth was, I wasn't sure what my opinion was. Listening to the morning debates at school, I knew I didn't agree completely with Tiffany, although I could see she had a point. I liked Brady's ideas more, but I couldn't say why.

"You know," I said finally, "I don't have much of an opinion about the gorillas. But I do have an opinion about the person who's making them."

"Really?" Eli leaned back against the counter. "Let's hear it."

"Okay, well, I was thinking about how someone decides to create something. I don't understand why he did it, but obviously there's thought and talent behind it, and it takes a kind of courage to do that, to just put something out there for everyone to judge."

"So you think he—or she—is courageous?"

"Yeah, I guess I do." I waited for more of a response from Eli. I wasn't used to blurting out my thoughts like that, and part of me worried that he'd laugh at me, but all he ended up saying was "Interesting."

A car pulled up, we filled the order and things were quiet for a few minutes until I broke the silence between us.

"Eli, do you think everyone is naturally creative?" It was something I'd been thinking about a lot lately. Everyone seemed to have something outside themselves that made them happy. Mom had her cakes and Lan had her orchids. I watched the other students at school, all of whom seemed to have something they loved, whether it was sports or music or movies. Even Tiffany Werner, with all of her pretentious flaws, had a passion for jewelry. Lately, I'd begun to feel like I was missing out on something. I didn't have anything, really, that I felt passionate about. I *liked* different things, but I didn't really *love* any one hobby or activity or distraction.

"I don't know if everyone has a creative outlet," Eli said, looking thoughtful. "But I think everyone should have something they love to do. I don't know if it has to be creative, though."

"Like sports?" I asked.

"Yeah. I mean, playing football isn't considered creative, really, but it does involve thought and feeling and dedication. That's an outlet of expression, right?"

"Right."

"Why do you ask?" He stood up in preparation for a car that had pulled into the parking lot. The driver was examining the menu posted just before the drive-through window.

"I dunno. It was just something I was thinking about. I don't really have anything like that."

"You make a great latte."

"Pouring liquid into a cup is not a talent," I muttered.

"There's got to be something you love."

I thought about all of the things I had tried to do in my life. There was ballet, but I wasn't graceful enough and it killed my toes. I took a ceramics course with Lan once, but painting chubby little animals didn't excite me. I tried music, but everyone told me I was tone-deaf. I couldn't draw a circle to save my life and any time I tried to help Mom decorate a cake I just made a huge mess.

"There's nothing I'm really good at," I said finally.

"Except precalculus," Eli said. "You really helped me out, you know?"

"Then why did you—" I stopped. Maybe I didn't want to know why he had changed around Trent. Maybe he didn't want to be associated with me, the sheriff's daughter. Maybe it was better to let it go and not think about it.

"Why did I what?" Eli looked puzzled. I had a hard time looking away from him. His eyes were the color of dark, polished wood.

"Nothing," I said. "It's nothing."

"Tell me."

I sighed. How do you ask a question when you don't want to know the answer? I tried to think of something clever, then blurted out the first thing that popped into my head.

"Lan likes Trent."

I immediately regretted my revelation. Lan would kill me if she knew. Eli looked both confused and shocked.

"Lan likes Trent?" he repeated.

"Please don't say anything to him," I begged.

Eli raised an eyebrow. "That could be a problem."

ON FRIDAY I DISCOVERED a shiny silver envelope in my locker, the corner edge peeking out from the grate where it had been slipped. My name looked like it had been laser-printed in a fancy font on the envelope. "Katherine Morgan" it read. On closer inspection, I realized that it was calligraphy, written by hand in deep blue ink.

I felt a surge of excitement, despite the fact that my name was wrong. It was an invitation to Tiffany's birthday party. I had just assumed there was no way I would be invited. She was still at war with my best friend, which I thought pretty much killed any chance I had of going. Tiffany and I had worked as lab partners during our sophomore year, but she barely spoke to me the entire semester except to inform me that she would not be cutting into dead frogs. Maybe the fact that I had completed the dissection lab by myself counted for something and she was paying me back with an invitation.

I grabbed the silver envelope and the books I needed for class, slammed my locker shut and hurried off to first period history.

"Guess what was in my locker this morning?" I said to Lan as I slid into my seat.

"Guess what was in everyone's locker this morning," Lan grumbled.

"You were invited? That's great!" I exclaimed happily.

"Look again. It's not what you think."

I carefully opened the envelope. The metallic pearl-colored paper was heavy in my hand, the exact opposite of the delicate cream-colored stationery folded inside. I read over the paper several times and then looked at Lan in confusion.

"It's an invitation to the invitation?"

Lan nodded. "She wants the entire school to show up in the parking lot next Tuesday just to see if they've been invited to her little soiree."

"What makes her think anyone's that desperate?"

"Well, the camera crew will be there, so I'm pretty sure she'll get a crowd."

I rolled my eyes and shoved the pseudoinvitation into my backpack. I looked around the room and saw other people examining their own silver envelopes, furrowing their brows and trying to make sense of them.

I hadn't told Lan yet that I had revealed her crush to Eli. I was hoping I wouldn't have to. Eli had sworn he wouldn't say anything to Trent, but he'd also said there was a problem.

"The thing is, Brady kind of likes Lan," he'd admitted.

"I thought Brady was dating a sophomore."

"He was. They broke up."

According to Eli, Trent would never date a girl if one of his friends liked her. It was some kind of loyalty code among guys. I told Eli I would try my best to get Lan to see the better qualities of Brady, but I wasn't making any promises.

"She really likes Trent," I said. "A lot."

"Well, Brady really likes her. A lot."

I decided that we needed to do whatever we could to make our friends happy, but Eli wanted to stay out of the way and let fate take its course.

"But what if fate needs a little nudge?" I asked.

"Fate never needs a nudge," Eli responded. "It only needs time."

I was still thinking about what Eli had said—*Fate only needs time*—when Tiffany stormed into class. She didn't look as happy as I would have expected the most incredibly popular girl at school to appear. In fact, she looked downright mad.

"Principal Carter is a complete moron," she announced to the class as she slammed her purse onto her desk. Mr. Gildea hadn't arrived yet, which was a good thing because there was no way he would tolerate her bashing the principal in his class, even if the complaint was remotely true.

Without waiting for anyone to ask *why* specifically Principal Carter was a complete moron, Tiffany dove into a bitter tirade.

"The camera crew wants to follow me around for one day. Just one day! They need some school footage," she explained as she furiously twirled a lock of hair. "But no, Carter says he can't have any more 'disruptions to the learning environment.' Can you believe that?"

I wasn't sure if we were supposed to respond or not. Most people were nodding sympathetically. After all, Tiffany was their ticket to a few golden minutes on national television. Her loss was our loss, I guessed.

Mr. Gildea walked in and began to take attendance. Tiffany sighed loudly, which Mr. Gildea ignored. "Time for our morning debate," he said. "Who would like to begin?"

Tiffany didn't bother to raise her hand. "It is grossly unjust that one man can prevent the national media from doing its job."

Mr. Gildea nodded. "Gross injustice is always a good topic," he said, trying to suppress a smile. I didn't think Tiffany realized he was poking fun at her.

"This is only the most socially significant event to occur in this town in a hundred years," Tiffany continued. "And for one man to attempt to destroy that…"

"How is your party being destroyed?" Brady interrupted. "It'll still be on TV. And isn't that what you want above all else? To cash in on your fifteen minutes of fame?"

He sounded annoyed, which was strange, because I was pretty sure that he was on the invitation list. Tiffany would want Trent to be there, and he never went anywhere without his friends. Invite Trent, and you invited them all.

Mr. Gildea jumped in before Tiffany and Brady could really go at it. "Let's focus on more historical examples of gross injustice," he said. "Turn to page thirty-four, please."

The rest of the day went by smoothly. Work was crazy because it was a Friday and for some reason people drink way more coffee on Friday than any other day—except for Monday morning, according to Bonnie. Eli's theory was that people wanted to be wide-awake when they went out on Friday night. My theory was that they were just treating themselves to something decadent—like our chocolate fudge brownie cappuccino—because it was the end of the workweek. We were debating this for the hundredth time when Bonnie came in.

"Hello, dears," she called out. Bonnie always came by on

Friday so she could take the day's money to the bank and lock up for the weekend.

"Eli, dear, does your brother still work for that sign company?" she asked.

Eli shook his head. "Not anymore. Ben's working at a lumberyard for a while."

Ben changed his major every semester, worked a new job every few months and spent his summers following bands around on tour. Eli said he was just trying to find himself. I thought he sounded a little scatterbrained.

"Hmm. Well, maybe I'll ask someone locally," Bonnie murmured.

"Are you getting a new sign?" I asked.

"I'd like to. Something a little more eye-catching, you know?"

Something's Brewing was the most unusual building in town, so I wasn't sure how Bonnie could make it more eye-catching unless she covered the place with Christmas lights and pink plastic flamingos. But I knew that once Bonnie decided upon something that was it. One way or another, Something's Brewing would stand out even more.

Bonnie and Eli were still talking when my dad arrived in his cruiser a half hour later. I was fully caffeinated and looking forward to the weekend as I sat in the front seat. I never sat in the back of my dad's police car. When I was a little kid I thought it was neat and would wave to people, but as I got older it became embarrassing. People always looked over at us while they waited at stoplights, and when they saw me sitting there behind the caged divider, I knew they thought I was some teenage drug addict or prostitute or something.

"How was your day?" Dad asked. His police scanner crackled as he pulled out of the parking lot.

"Pretty good."

"Anything interesting happen?"

"Nope."

"Your classes are good?"

"Yep."

My dad and I had the same conversation nearly every day. I don't know what he expected me to say. School was school. Each day was pretty much like the one before unless it was the day before a vacation, in which case everything was crazy. Still, I tried to give him at least one detail so he'd feel like we were actually talking instead of just reciting the same words over and over.

"I got a ninety on my English essay," I told him. "I think I'll get an A this semester."

"That's nice," he said. I could tell he was distracted by something because he slowed down a little and kept glancing to the left.

"Yeah. It's too bad I'm failing all my other classes," I joked.

"Well, good," he said. He wasn't paying attention anymore. I wondered what had caught his eye. Suddenly, he made a sharp left and sped up. I braced my arm against the door.

"Whoa," I said. "What's going on?"

Dad didn't answer because he was barking numbers into his police scanner. He turned abruptly again, this time into the parking lot of Cleary Dry Cleaners. I panicked when I saw what we were doing there: a group of six kids wearing hoodie jackets was spray-painting the side of the building. I slouched down in my seat, hoping they weren't kids from school and that they wouldn't see me.

Dad turned on the flashing lights.

"Wait here," he said.

He got out of the car and approached the kids. I thought for sure they would have started running as soon as they saw the cop car, but they were frozen in place. I peered over the dashboard to get a better look at them and was relieved that not one of them was tall enough to be any of the boys I knew from school. In fact, they were all short. Middle-school short. I sat up straighter. Was it possible that these little kids were responsible for the gorillas?

I looked over at the brick wall. They had been trying to paint a gorilla, but it was nowhere near as good as the ones at school. "Copycats," I murmured.

A few minutes later, two more squad cars pulled up and Dad let the new officers handle the situation. He shook his head as we headed home.

"I don't think those kids will be out spray-painting again any time soon," he said.

"Did you scare them?" I asked.

Dad chuckled. "I think so. They were young, not even thirteen. We'll call their parents. I think that might be punishment enough."

I was relieved that my classmates had not been involved, but mad that my dad had taken me along with him. What if it *had* been kids I knew? Mom would freak if she found out. She always anticipated the worst, like gangs with knives hidden in their pants. Dad seemed to know what I was thinking.

"I'm sorry about that," he said. "I shouldn't have involved you."

I nodded. "I'll tell Mom. I think that will be punishment enough."

He smiled. "Any way we can leave Mom out of it? Name your price."

I pretended to think about it, but I already knew what I wanted. "Driving lessons," I told him. "And I want to drive Mom's car, not the cruiser."

Dad sighed. "I don't know."

I shrugged. "Okay. I have my cell right here. Maybe I'll just call Mom…"

"Fine. You got me. Three driving lessons. That's all."

I settled into my seat, satisfied. As we drove home I thought more about the graffiti. The person responsible was still out there, and I wondered when—and where—the gorillas would appear next.

MOM ASKED ME TO HELP OUT at Cleary Confections the next day. One of her assistants had called in sick, and when that happened Mom usually asked me to take over the cash register so she could focus on the baking. Lan came with me, too. Mom always paid us in cash at the end of the day, and we both loved that.

"I'm up to my neck in birthday cakes," she told us when we got there. She was wearing her white baker's apron and had her hair tucked under a little net. "And Saturdays are always busiest in the morning. Thanks for your help, girls."

I liked helping out at the bakery. It smelled warm and sweet and the customers were usually in a good mood. I ran the register while Lan made sure the glass cases were stocked with delicate pastries, colorful cookies and plump fruit pies. We were able to talk and snack and just sit back when things slowed down, and sometimes I took pictures of the especially decorative cakes for Mom.

People tended to arrive in a sudden wave and everything would be hectic for an hour, then the store would be quiet and empty for a while. It was always like that, almost as if the customers planned it that way. It was during one of those vacant periods that Lan brought up something I hadn't even thought of yet.

"So will your mom be making Tiffany's birthday cake?"

Instead of answering her, I nearly ran to the back room. Lan was right behind me. We found my mom bent over a sheet cake, piping thick white frosting into a shell pattern around the sides.

"Mom, are you making Tiffany Werner's birthday cake?" I asked.

She looked up, startled. "No, this is for the senior center."

"Her birthday is in March."

"Oh, Kate, I have no idea. I'm doing all I can to stay focused on this weekend. You can check my planner, though."

Lan and I rushed to the little office in the back and flipped through the leather planning book that sat on Mom's desk.

"What's the date again?" I asked.

"March 3."

I found the page for Saturday, March 3. There were two wedding cakes scheduled, three anniversary sheet cakes and a toddler's birthday cake, which, according to the message next to it, was to be shaped like a baby whale. Mom had slapped a yellow Post-it note on the page. "Date is full—no more orders."

"What a relief," I said, closing the planner. "Even if Tiffany wanted a cake, they won't take her order. They're doing two weddings that day and I'm sure Tiffany's cake would be more work than those two put together."

Mom never scheduled more than two wedding cakes in a single day because they took forever to decorate and she had to deliver them herself.

"Can you imagine if your mom was invited to the party and you weren't?" Lan asked with a short laugh. "That would be so awful."

"I just don't want her to have to work for the Werners," I said, rolling my eyes. "They'd probably treat her like a servant and complain about every minute detail."

We returned to the front room, which was still empty, sat down at one of the little café tables and treated ourselves to buttercream cupcakes.

"The invitation ceremony is on Tuesday," Lan said, pulling the paper off her cupcake.

I corrected her with a smile. "The invitation celebration."

Lan shook her head. "I hate myself for wanting to go, but I do. This will be bigger than the prom. And did you hear? She's getting Nothing Serious to play."

Nothing Serious were a local band, but they had recently opened for some big names and were going to be putting out a CD on a major label soon.

"I know," I said. "It sounds great. But then again, it's going to be all about Tiffany. She'll probably sit on a throne and make people bow or chant her name or something."

Lan shrugged and took a bite of her cupcake. I knew how much she wanted to go, in part because everyone would be talking about it and in part because Trent would be there. But there seemed to be more to it than that, something she wasn't telling me.

"So why do you really want to go?" I asked as gently as I could.

Lan put her cupcake down on a napkin. "Do you know how many times I've been asked if I'm Chinese or Japanese?" she asked.

I didn't, but I had an idea. I'd been with her many times when it had happened, and she always answered, "I'm Vietnamese-American." Her parents had both been born in Vietnam, but she had been born in Cleary.

"Or how many times people have referred to me as Oriental?" she continued.

I had made that mistake once, too. She told me that *Oriental* only applied to objects, like lamps or rugs. People were Asian, not Oriental.

"The point is, I'm always kind of on the outside, you know? My dad is pretty traditional, my friends are almost all American, and I fall somewhere in between. I don't think anyone sees me as one of them."

I began to protest, but she shook her head. "I don't mean you, Kate. But everyone else…" Her voice trailed off. "I just thought that if I was invited to this party it would mean something."

"Like what?"

"I don't know. It would mean that I was just like everybody else, you know?" Her voice was soft and she stared at her half-eaten cupcake instead of looking at me.

I did know, in a way. I knew that my friend was hurting and that she wanted something badly. I felt sort of helpless. What could I do? I knew what would make Lan happy, but I had no way to get it for her.

We were bombarded with customers around noon, and Mom had to deliver one of the cakes, so we stayed busy for a while, but the entire time I was ringing orders up all I could think about was a way to get Lan an invitation to Tiffany's birthday party. If she wanted to go, I told myself,

I would do everything I could to help her. Even if it meant sucking up to Tiffany Werner.

THE PARTY CAME UP AGAIN as I ate dinner with my parents that night.

"By the way, why were you and Lan so interested in my orders earlier?" Mom asked. She had finished icing her cakes on time, her customers were happy and she was in a good mood.

"Oh, that. There's this girl from school who's having a huge birthday party in March. We just wanted to see if you were making the cake."

"Am I?"

"Nope. You are not making Tiffany Werner's cake."

Dad looked at me. "Did you say Werner?"

I froze with my fork in midair. "Yeah."

"Is she having her party at the country club?"

I knew what he was going to say. My mom might not be going to the party, but my dad would be.

"You're handling the security, aren't you?" I asked miserably.

"Not exactly. They're hiring a private security company. But the manager of the country club asked me to keep officers in the area." He raised an eyebrow at Mom. "Apparently, this is a very big party and he's afraid that the kids might get out of hand. We'll be keeping an eye on the roads."

"Are you going, Kate?" Mom asked.

"I don't think so," I said. "The invite list is kind of exclusive."

Mom cleared her throat. "I see. Well, you don't want to go to a party like that anyway, do you?"

I shrugged. My social standing at Cleary High School was not something I wanted to discuss with my parents at dinner. I also did not want them feeling sorry for me. There's nothing worse than parental pity.

"You could have your own party here," Dad suggested.

I groaned. Their intentions were good, but my parents had no clue. "Thanks, but I think I'll be fine. Lan's probably not invited, either, so we'll just hang out that weekend."

"Well, that's nice," Mom said. She and Dad exchanged a meaningful glance at one another and then tactfully changed the subject to taxes and W-2 forms and other completely boring matters, so I tuned them out.

After dinner I went upstairs and downloaded pictures from my camera. I'd taken more than I'd realized, snapping shots here and there throughout the week. I created a new file, then pulled it up so I could watch a slide show of the images.

Most of the pictures were of Lan, but I'd also taken some around school and outside. Eden Alder had asked me to take a picture of her sitting at the newspaper table, and I'd taken one of Trent standing on top of his car. I e-mailed that one to Lan.

I thought about Lan and the party. I wanted to go just to see the spectacle and so I could say I was there, but at the same time, I didn't want to feed Tiffany's obese ego. Did an invitation mean that I actually belonged to something? Or did it simply tag me as a sheep in Tiffany's ever-growing flock?

I wanted Eli's take on it. He was always able to express his thoughts more clearly than I could. And he was so comfortable with himself. It was as if he never questioned who he was or what his place was within the world, or at least his place within the tiny universe of Cleary. Would I ever be that comfortable in my own skin? I often worried that my shirt was out of style or that someone would point out that I'd worn the same pair of jeans to school twice in one week.

I deleted some of the blurry pictures and tried to lighten some of the darker ones. The last picture on my screen was of Eli. I'd forgotten I'd even taken it. I had been testing my camera at Something's Brewing, trying to see if the red-eye remover button actually worked, and I'd asked Eli to look up from his computer. As soon as he turned in my direction, I'd snapped the picture.

Looking at the image on my screen, I smiled. I had caught Eli off guard, and he looked startled. Even with his surprised expression and disheveled hair, he was cute. Not that he'd care if I told him that.

People like Eli and Trent and Brady seemed naturally impervious to the opinions of others. They could speak up in class and not be afraid that someone would snicker or mock them. People like me, on the other hand, always questioned themselves. What if my opinion was wrong? What if someone challenged me and I couldn't defend my own thoughts? It was better to keep your mouth shut and listen, I decided. If only Lan had done the same thing and not jumped into the debate against Tiffany in history class, maybe she would have a chance at being invited to the party.

But I knew Lan better than that. If she had something to say, she said it. After what she told me the other day, I wondered if she had learned early on to stand up for herself, to define herself to others before they could sling their stereotypes at her.

I turned off my computer. "Stupid party," I muttered. How had one meticulously organized event been able to cause so much turmoil? And part of me knew that it wasn't over.

The chaos was just beginning.

THE STUDENT BODY OF Cleary High School was completely consumed with the impending invitation ceremony, a real live camera crew and, of course, Tiffany Werner herself, who attracted gasps and stares wherever she went. She pretended not to notice, but I knew Tiffany was relishing every second of the undivided attention. The mysterious graffiti paled in comparison to a nationally televised sixteenth birthday extravaganza, so we put the gorillas out of our minds.

Apparently, they didn't do the same with us.

The day before Tiffany's "invitation celebration," which she actually advertised with a half-page ad in the *Cleary Chronicle*—Find Out if You've Been Chosen was the headline, done in a formal, flowery script above a professional photo of Tiffany wearing a diamond tiara and a wide, toothy smile—another gorilla appeared in town. This time, it was painted on the side of an old bank with the caption "When money speaks, the truth keeps silent." The gorilla was identical to the ones on the side of our school. I was confused. After our school had been painted, the gorillas had moved out of state. Had the person responsible returned to Cleary? And if so, why?

News of the gorilla sparked yet another morning debate in Mr. Gildea's class, with Tiffany taking the position that all graffiti was simply an illegal waste of time and Brady arguing that freedom of expression should not be limited to pen and paper. Then another guy jumped in, saying that the gorilla actually helped draw attention to an abandoned and neglected building.

"Maybe the city will finally do something about it," he said.

The bank had been empty for years and now mainly served as a place to park and make out behind. Kevin and I had gone there once a week when we were dating. The thought made me feel lonely. It wasn't that I missed Kevin. I missed being part of a couple, having someone to sit close to and talk to and feel warm with.

The debate went back and forth for a while until Mr. Gildea said it was time to wrap it up. "Final thoughts," he announced. I was waiting for Lan to say something. I knew she was trying to stay out of it so she wouldn't offend Tiffany and ruin her chances of getting an invitation, but I also knew she was dying to join in the discussion.

Brady raised his hand. "Simply because someone's art hasn't been sanctioned by the government does not make it illegal or insignificant," he said. People nodded. Brady had a way of making things sound good.

Tiffany sighed loudly. "Just because someone has freedom of expression does not mean they have freedom to ruin or destroy someone else's property."

Lan finally jumped in. "Painting something does not ruin or destroy it," she said, keeping her voice calm. I caught a glimpse of Brady beaming at her. He no longer sat in the back; instead, he had moved several desks closer to my best friend. I wondered if she'd noticed.

We moved on to a chapter review, but the debate stayed with me throughout the day. I brought it up with Eli at work.

We had just filled a huge order of over a dozen different

drinks for a guy in a business suit. He watched us closely and demanded that we double-check all the lids to make sure they were on tight. I figured he was taking them back to his office and was afraid they might spill all over the leather interior of his tiny silver sports car.

"What do you think about all of this?" I asked.

"I think cars like that are a desperate attempt to cover up issues of male inadequacy," Eli said. He was on his computer, typing an essay for English.

"No, not that. The gorillas. What do you think about the new gorillas?"

"I don't know. They're cool, I guess." He frowned. "I think my spell-checker is wrong."

"Spell-checker is never wrong."

Eli was preoccupied with his paper, so I gave up trying to have a meaningful conversation with him and returned to cleaning the espresso machine. Bonnie said I did the best job, but I suspected she was just using flattery to get me to complete the most undesirable task at Something's Brewing.

After I got home from work I flopped onto my bed and called Lan. She and Eli were in the same English class and Lan was also working on her paper.

"I can't believe it's due tomorrow,' she said. "Five full pages! I'll never be able to fill five pages with stuff about American Romanticism."

"Does Eli talk a lot during class?" I asked. I rolled onto my back and looked up at the ceiling. Years earlier Lan and I had spent hours positioning little plastic stars across the white plaster to resemble some of the constellations. At night, they would glow a faint green color that I found oddly soothing.

"Are you asking if he talks to other people? Not really." I could hear the clicking of her computer keys as she typed.

"No, I mean, does he speak up during discussions, that kind of thing?"

"Yeah, if he's got something to say. Right now he seems to think that Thoreau and Whitman are gods."

"Really? He likes Whitman?" I noticed a few of the larger stars were coming loose, so I stood on my bed and pressed at them with the palm of my hand.

"Yeah, he's always quoting one thing or another." The typing stopped. "Wait a minute. Why are you asking about Eli?"

I froze, my hand planted against a star. "No reason. I mean, we work together and I was just curious. That's all."

Lan laughed. "I knew it. I just knew it. You have a crush on Eli!"

I felt my face burn red. It wasn't a big deal, but I didn't like how Lan thought it was so funny. I sat back down on my bed.

"Forget it," I said. "I'll talk to you tomorrow. Good luck on your paper."

"Don't hang up! Kate, I'm sorry I was laughing. I think it's great. I think you guys would be perfect together, really."

"It doesn't matter," I said. "He's with Reva."

"You could take her," Lan joked.

"She could tear off half my face with those nails of hers," I muttered. "Besides, he just sees me as a friend. Not even that. I'm a coworker, that's all."

"You know, I don't think things are going all that well with Eli and Reva," Lan said.

I felt a little spark of hope. "What makes you say that?"

"She was out in the hallway after class a few days ago and

they started arguing." Lan was typing again and I knew she had to get back to work, but I wanted some details.

"What were they arguing about?"

"I didn't hear all of it. I was on my way out," Lan said. "But I know he said that he needed more space."

"Interesting."

We were quiet for a moment. The clicking of the keyboard was slow, like a metronome, and I closed my eyes.

"It would be so great if you started dating Eli," Lan said.

"Yeah."

"I mean, it would be great for me, too. I would get more time with Trent. We could all hang out together."

I was tempted to tell Lan about Brady's crush, but I had promised Eli I wouldn't say anything, so I kept my mouth shut. Lan gushed for a few minutes about Trent before I reminded her that she had a paper due.

"Ugh. I'm only on page two and I am totally out of ideas," she complained.

"'Whatever satisfies the soul is truth,'" I recited automatically.

"What's that?"

"A quote by Whitman. It's one of my favorites."

Lan groaned. "You sound like Eli."

I smiled and looked up at the plastic stars. "That's not such a bad thing," I said.

IT WAS JUST LIKE THE FIRST DAY of school. The crowded parking lot, the cell phones held high, the excited rumbling of hundreds of students. This time, they weren't looking at the wall, even though the gorillas were still there. This time, all eyes were focused on Tiffany Werner as she stood on a wide wooden stool looking out over the crowd, dressed in a white overcoat and matching gloves, a sparkling tiara perched on her head. Her two best friends, Monica and Mallory, positioned themselves on either side, smirking a little at the horde of people.

Tiffany held up a bullhorn. Behind her, a cameraman filmed the crowd while another guy held a fluffy microphone above Tiffany's head. A third cameraman stood off to the side, his lens trained on Tiffany.

"I will now call out the names of the chosen," she announced, her expression serious. "Once your name has been called, please come up here to receive your invitation."

Lan and I stood against the back wall, our backpacks on the pavement at out feet. It was going to be impossible to get past the crowd to Lan's car, so we decided to wait it out for a while and watch the drama unfold before our eyes.

"This is so stupid," I muttered. I pulled my digital camera out of my backpack and snapped pictures of the crowd and the camera crew. I took a few of Tiffany, too. She looked strangely artificial to me as she stood there in her fake crown, surrounded by people paid to capture her every word on film.

Tiffany cleared her throat and began reading the names aloud.

"Marcus Abbott," she called. People clapped when one of their friends went up to receive an invitation from either Monica or Mallory, who seemed to be taking their duty very seriously. When Tiffany called Trent Adams, people looked around, but he was nowhere in sight.

"If she thought Trent was going to stand in line for an invitation, she's seriously deluded," Lan remarked.

When Trent didn't appear, Tiffany moved on to the next name, but I could tell she was mad because she sighed a little, and it echoed through the bullhorn. She expected everyone to treat her ridiculous ceremony with the same reverence one would reserve for a royal coronation.

"Let's go," I said as the crowd began to thin out. Tiffany was halfway through the alphabet and people were starting to realize that they weren't on the list. I heard Eli's name called, but he was another no-show.

It was chilly, and I shoved my hands into my coat pockets. It never got really cold in Cleary, and I had only seen snow three times in my whole life, so I had a low tolerance for winter weather.

"Kate Morgan."

Lan grabbed my arm. It took me a moment to understand why she was pulling at me. Tiffany had just called my name.

"Kate Morgan?"

People were looking at me. Someone was pushing me forward until I was standing in front of Monica and Mallory. Monica handed me a small blue box while Mallory checked my name off a typed list. I must have looked completely confused, because Tiffany began to giggle. "You can go now. Congratulations."

I turned around and searched for Lan. I didn't see her but figured she had headed to her car, so I walked toward the other end of the parking lot with the blue box jammed inside my coat pocket. I found Lan sitting in her car with the heater on at full blast.

"Can you believe it?" I asked as I slid into the passenger seat. I pulled the invitation from my pocket. It was a little bigger than a ring box and "Tiffany-blue." Lan was silent as I flipped back the lid. Inside was a blue plastic bracelet and a piece of paper folded into a diamond shape. I carefully unfolded the cream-colored stationery and read it aloud, being careful not to sound excited. I already knew that if Lan wasn't going, neither was I. There was no way I would choose some party over my best friend. Ever.

"You have been chosen to celebrate Tiffany Werner's sixteenth birthday on Saturday, March 3 at the Cleary Country Club. Please arrive between 7:00 and 7:30 p.m. Tiffany will make her entrance at 8:00 p.m. sharp. No one will be admitted after that time. All guests must wear the bracelet provided. Only those invited may attend—no uninvited dates. Formal dress. Guests may not wear blue or white."

I turned to Lan, who was just staring out the window watching the crowd slowly drift away.

"Can you believe her? I've never heard of someone telling people what they can't wear."

Lan didn't answer.

"Lan?"

"You should go," she said finally.

I thought she was telling me to get out of the car. "Lan, I had no idea that Tiffany was going to invite me! I don't know why she did, honest! Please don't be mad!"

Lan looked at me. "I'm not mad at you, Kate. I'm saying that you should go to the party."

I folded my arms across my chest. "Nope. No way. Not without you."

"Well, I'm not going to be invited without divine intervention." She sighed and looked out the window again. Only a few kids and the camera crew remained. "I hate the fact that this means something to me," she murmured.

"I'm not going," I said again. "You and I will do something fun that weekend instead."

Lan gave me a sad smile. "You say that now, but this is going to be the only thing anyone talks about for a month. You'll want to go and I won't blame you. You should go. Then you can tell me all about it." She pretended to wipe dust off her dashboard.

"I can tell you about it now," I said. "Tiffany will wear a ridiculously expensive dress, she'll arrive on the back of a unicorn or something, and everyone will have to stand around and clap any time she sneezes. No thanks."

Lan began to protest, but I held up my hand. "I'm not going. End of discussion. Now take me to work, please."

I was only a few minutes late to Something's Brewing, so I

knew Bonnie wouldn't mind. I invited Lan inside for a cappuccino and she said okay. When we got inside, Eli was there with Brady.

"Sorry I'm late," I said as I took off my coat. "Traffic was crazy. The parking lot was jammed."

Brady was staring at Lan, but she didn't seem to notice. Eli did, though, and he winked at me. I tried not to smile as I made Lan an almond cappuccino, her favorite.

"Right. The invitation thing was today," Eli said.

"Yes, and I heard your name called, so you'll have to get your invitation from Tiffany tomorrow."

Eli rolled his eyes. "Yeah, I'll be sure to do that."

"You don't want to go?" asked Lan. I noticed that Brady had inched forward and was standing right next to her, which wasn't difficult to do in the small space of Something's Brewing. Her long black hair contrasted with Brady's pale blond, closely cropped cut.

"No. She only invited me because Trent said she had to or he wasn't coming."

"Were you invited?" Lan asked Brady. I couldn't remember if his name had been called or not.

"Uh, yeah. I mean, I think so. I don't know," Brady stammered. He was actually blushing a little. "Are you going?" he asked Lan. She just shook her head no. I handed her the cappuccino and tried to think of a way to change the subject. Eli beat me to it.

"So thanks to the math whiz here, I passed my precalc test," he said.

"Good. Maybe you can get that car and I can stop driving you around everywhere," Brady joked.

"But I just love having a chauffeur," Eli said. Lan laughed and Brady smiled and we were all quiet for one awkward moment. Then a car pulled up to the window and Lan and Brady had to move back because there was so little room.

"I'll talk to you later, Kate," said Lan as she left.

Brady followed her out and, as I made change for a crumpled twenty-dollar bill, I saw through the window that they were both standing next to Lan's car, talking.

"That's a good sign," I said softly.

Eli leaned over me to get a look. "Good," he said. Again, I caught the faint scent of his soap and something minty on his breath. I closed my eyes for just a second to breathe it in, then moved away.

Our customer left and Eli pulled out his laptop while I went over to the sink. "I meant what I said earlier," he commented while the computer warmed up.

"What's that?" I was rinsing off one of the long-handled spoons we used to stir steamed milk.

"You helped me pass that precalc test. Thanks."

"No problem." I was thinking about Lan and Brady. If they did start dating, it would probably mean double dates with Eli and Reva, and I was pretty sure I wouldn't be coming along. I tried to think of some of the other eligible guys in their group, but no one with potential came to mind.

"You still following the graffiti story?" Eli asked.

I sat down in a folding chair across from him and leaned back. "Not really. I guess I've been a little distracted by this party."

"Oh. I didn't think you wanted to go to that," Eli said. He didn't look up from his computer, but there was something in his voice that bothered me. It sounded like he was disappointed, but I couldn't imagine why.

"I don't. But Lan does."

"Would you go if she was going?"

"Probably."

Eli finally looked up from the computer. "Why?"

I shrugged. "I don't know. Because it's big. Because everyone will be there. Because it's going to be on TV."

"Hmm."

"What? Aren't you going?" I was starting to get annoyed.

"Nope."

"Why not?"

"Because it's big. Because everyone will be there. Because it's going to be on TV."

"Very funny," I said. "So basically you're above everyone who wants to go?"

He smiled. "I didn't say I was above everyone else."

I was suddenly irritated by Eli's smile. It appeared smug. There was nothing wrong with wanting to attend a big party, even if you didn't like the hostess. There was nothing wrong with wanting to be social and get along with people and have fun. Eli seemed to be hinting that there was.

"If you don't want to go, then don't go," I said. "But you don't have to make other people feel like they are inherently flawed and somehow inferior just because they want to see what all the fuss is about."

I got up and stormed to the back room. Eli had no right to criticize me. He could sit there and convince everyone he was a nonconformist, and that was fine. But he had no right to judge others. I shut the door and slumped against the wall next to a metal shelf stacked with paper cups and tall bottles of flavored coffee syrup. The storeroom had that weird cardboard smell to it. I could hear Eli taking someone's order and I didn't feel the least bit guilty for making him work alone.

After ten minutes, Eli knocked softly on the storeroom door.

"You okay?"

I didn't answer. Let him wonder, I thought. Let him worry a little.

"Can I bring you something? Water? Juice? A weapon of some sort?"

I chuckled at that, and I knew he heard me. I opened the door a crack, but remained sitting on the floor. Eli hunched down on the other side of the door so that we were almost face-to-face.

"Sorry I upset you," he said. "I seem to have a real talent for doing that."

"Yes, you do," I agreed. I paused for a moment. "Or maybe I have a talent for taking everything the wrong way."

"Can we call a truce?" He held out his hand. I took it. It was warm and smooth. He helped pull me to my feet, and we returned to the front of the store.

"Are you going to tell me what's really bothering you?" Eli asked. "I know it can't all be me."

"It isn't," I said. "But sometimes I feel like you're really harsh on people who don't think exactly the way you do."

He nodded. "I get that. It's just that there are some things I feel strongly about, you know? And I want other people to feel the same."

"Well, maybe you need to try a new approach," I said, but I smiled so he would know I wasn't trying to be mean.

He smiled back. "So, what else is bothering you?"

I could tell he wasn't going to let it go until I came clean, so I did. I told him about why Tiffany's party meant so much to Lan and how I was still struggling to find something that I was good at that wasn't math- or coffee-related. Eli seemed to listen to me as I rattled on for a few minutes. He nodded and asked questions. When I was finished, he was quiet for a moment before he spoke.

"I think I can help you," he said.

A brash voice interrupted Eli before he could say any more. "Help her with what?"

We turned around, startled. We hadn't heard the back door open, so neither one of us knew how long Reva had been standing there listening to our conversation. Not that we were doing anything wrong, but suddenly I felt embarrassed and guilty.

"Hi, Reva," Eli said. I smiled and gave her a little half wave. I didn't know what to say.

Reva walked over and stood next to Eli, planting a kiss on his cheek and tracing her finger over his ear. "Help her with what?" she asked again. She wasn't wearing her usual spiky heels, I noticed, which was probably why we hadn't heard her.

Eli cleared his throat and moved away. I could tell he didn't like having his ear tickled. "We were talking about helping Lan get an invitation to Tiffany Werner's birthday party."

Reva snorted. "She can have mine. I'm not going anywhere near that freak show."

Eli gave me a sympathetic look as if to apologize for Reva, who was now studying one of her long silver fingernails.

"I wish it was that easy," I said, "but there's a guest list and even if you have a bracelet, security won't let you in if your name's not on the list."

Reva shrugged. "Oh, well. No big deal." She turned her back to me and faced Eli. "When do you get off from work?"

"I'll be done in about an hour," Eli said.

Reva sighed. "I am not hanging out here for a full hour," she complained. "Can't you leave just a little bit early? Please? I'm sure Katie won't mind."

"It's Kate," I said, but Reva acted like she hadn't heard me.

"Why don't you come back in an hour?" Eli asked.

"I can't. If you want a ride, you have to come with me now."

I busied myself at the sink while Reva and Eli went back and forth about the ride situation. They walked to the storeroom, where they lowered their voices so I couldn't hear them.

A minivan pulled up to the window. It was the same mom from the week before, and the backseat was full of howling kids. "Can I get five apple juices and a double espresso?" she asked as she dug through her purse.

"Uh, sure," I said, glancing toward the storeroom. I needed Eli to help me but was unsure if I should bother him. One of the kids in the van leaned over his mom and honked the horn and she began yelling at him. Eli stuck his head out the door.

"Need help?" he asked.

I nodded and began pulling down cups for the juice. Eli joined me, and we had the order ready within five minutes.

"Sorry," I said. "I didn't mean to interrupt your conversation. Looks like we're all clear now."

I heard a car peel out of the parking lot and caught a glimpse of Reva behind the wheel of a black sedan, speeding away.

"I'm really sorry, Eli," I said. "I didn't mean to cause a problem between you and—"

"Forget it," he interrupted. "She's wound a little tight right now. It's not you."

"What about your ride?"

He raised an eyebrow at me. "Well, looks like I need a favor."

I don't know why I felt my heart flutter a little, but it did. Not that it meant anything.

7

THERE IS NOTHING MORE AWFUL, more cringe-worthy or more makes-you-wish-you-were-suddenly-invisible than having your dad pick you up in a police car. It might be worse if he picked you up in, say, a hearse with a fresh coffin in the back. Maybe. But a police car is pretty much at the top of the list when it comes to the worst possible ways to take a guy home. A hearse might have a creepy-cool vibe. A police car? Creepy-uncool vibe. I warned Eli ahead of time.

"We'll have to sit in the back," I said. "We'll look like criminals." I glanced out the window, expecting Dad to pull in at any moment.

"It won't be the first time," he said. I must have looked shocked, because he laughed. "Kidding."

Dad arrived and I introduced him to Eli, who was extremely polite, but I saw Dad smirk when I slid into the backseat. As we pulled out of the front of the parking lot, I noticed Reva's car turning into the back. I didn't say anything, though.

At first, the drive was uncomfortably quiet. Dad asked Eli some questions about how to get to his house, but that was all. The police scanner buzzed and crackled, and we could hear the dispatcher's voice reciting numbers and codes in her calm, stoic voice. After one of these announcements, though, Dad perked up.

"Huh," he said.

"What is it?" I wondered if there was any chance he would drag us on a high-speed chase, but I knew he would never go over the speed limit with two "civilian minors" in the car.

"Sounds like they've discovered another mural." He turned right at the next light. "Mind if we take a look?"

I glanced at Eli, who nodded. "Okay," I said, even though it was definitely not okay. What if there were kids there? Worse, what if this time they were kids we knew? I closed my eyes and willed Dad to change his mind and drive us straight to Eli's house. No such luck. I slid down in the seat a little and hoped Eli didn't notice me turning red with embarrassment.

We slowed down in front of a tuxedo rental place with a huge going-out-of-business banner draped across the front. I didn't see the gorilla at first, but then Dad turned the corner, and there it was, four feet high and just like the others. "They call this a monkey suit" was painted above the gorilla's head. I laughed out loud. Eli grinned.

There was already another police car there, and Dad pulled up alongside it and talked to the officer behind the wheel. The other officer frowned at us, but when he recognized me, he smiled and waved.

"I hope you don't do this to all Kate's boyfriends," he remarked to my dad. I was horrified. I looked over at Eli, who was just gazing out the window, smiling.

"He's not—" I began to say, but Dad interrupted and asked the officer about the gorilla.

"The owner just discovered it," the officer said. "It must have been done last night, but no one parks on this side, so he didn't see it this morning. Same as the others."

Dad nodded. "That's what? Three now?"

"Yeah. The school, the bank and now this. We found some spray-paint cans in the Dumpster out back. We'll check 'em for prints, but if this guy is clever, he wiped 'em clean."

"I'm guessing he's clever," Dad said, "but check anyway. Thanks, George."

I made a mental note to myself that George was to be avoided at all costs in the future.

We pulled away from the store. "It's just the darndest thing," Dad said. I wasn't sure if he was talking to us or just talking out loud.

"What's that, Dad?"

"Well, we got a report last night that one of these gorillas was spotted in Oklahoma. They e-mailed us a picture and it's the exact same thing. But that's hundreds of miles away. There's no way the same person could have done both within the same day, but they're absolutely identical."

"Sounds like it's more than one person," I said.

Eli was rummaging through his backpack, not really paying attention to us. I hoped he wasn't trying to avoid talking to me. I hoped even more that he didn't think I had told my dad we were dating. I knew my face was still red and I was kind of glad Eli wasn't looking at me.

"It just doesn't make sense," Dad continued. "Why would one person focus the graffiti on three buildings in Cleary while another paints them in different towns and different states?" He sighed. "Are the kids talking about this at school?"

I glanced at Eli, horrified that Dad was breaking our don't-ask-don't-tell policy in front of him. "We have a deal, remember?"

"Sorry, Kate," he said. "You, too, Eli. Forget I mentioned it."

"No problem, Mr. Morgan," Eli said, zippering his backpack. I don't think he even knew what my dad was apologizing for. "Turn here. I'm the third one on the left."

We pulled into the driveway of a two-story brick colonial. It was your basic ordinary house, with bright blue shutters and a topiary on the front porch shaped like three balls sitting on top of one another. It wasn't the kind of place I thought Eli would live in, but what did I expect? Something painted black with a big red anarchy sign splashed across the garage?

"Thanks for the ride," Eli said as he got out. "See you tomorrow, Kate."

"Bye," I said, hoping he didn't think I was completely idiotic.

I watched him as he walked up to the front door. He reached into his front pocket and retrieved a key. Dad pulled away, and I turned my head so I could watch Eli go into his house.

"Nice boy," Dad said.

"Yeah."

"How long have you known him?"

"Since sophomore year. We had English together."

"He seems nice."

"You said that."

If Dad was waiting for me to confess that I had a hidden crush on Eli, he was going to be waiting a long time. I did not discuss boys with my parents. Ever.

"I think I did pretty well on my history paper," I said, trying to keep my voice nonchalant. I wanted to talk about anything but Eli.

Dad smiled. "I guess that means you like him."

"Huh?"

"You always talk about school so you won't have to talk about the boys you like."

He made it sound like I had a hundred crushes, like I was always swooning over some guy.

"He has a girlfriend," I said.

"Okay."

"He's off-limits."

"Right." Dad nodded like he understood, but I knew he didn't. I tried changing the subject again.

"So do you think the gorilla graffiti will make another appearance?" I asked.

Dad sighed. "Yes. Our guy's smart. And he's talented, and he seems to enjoy it. We'll catch him, I think. Just need some more time."

I gazed out the window as we passed trees and houses and made our way to the main road. "What does it all mean?" I murmured.

"What's that?"

"I wonder what they mean, the gorillas. What's the message? What's the point?"

"No point," Dad said. "Just some prankster having fun. Don't read too much into it, Kate."

I hoped that Eli didn't read too much into George's little comment or think that I drove around with my dad all the time, checking out crime scenes. I didn't know what he thought of me, exactly, but I was pretty sure that he was not looking at me as potential girlfriend material.

Mom was waiting for us when we got home. She wanted to have an early dinner because she had to get back to work to deal with some cake-related emergency.

"Honestly, Sam should be handling this," she said after we sat down. She was still wearing her white apron. Little blotches of blue icing were smeared across it.

"Did you tell him that?" Dad asked, his mouth half-full of pot roast.

"How do you tell your boss that you don't want to do your job?"

"You just said it wasn't your job."

"It shouldn't be, but I handle all the cakes, so technically it is." Mom sighed. "We have limits for a reason. It's just not possible to fill this order."

I poked at a mushy carrot with my fork. Sometimes I liked to hear my parents discuss work, particularly if they were talking about coworkers they didn't like. I didn't think adults talked about other people the same way my friends and I did in the cafeteria, but gossip seemed to cross generations.

"And how was your day, Kate?" Mom asked.

"Fine."

"We took one of Kate's, uh, *friends* home." Dad cleared his throat and I glanced up to see him give Mom one of those meaningful parental looks they thought I never noticed.

"He's just someone I work with," I said. "That's it."

Mom nodded. "And what is his name?" Her smile was a little too wide, like she thought it was all very cute that I liked a guy.

I stabbed at an overdone potato chunk, mashing it in half. "Eli. His name is Eli. And I don't want to talk about him."

"I see." I knew my parents were exchanging their look again, but I ignored them, and the conversation turned to their weekend plan to buy a new sofa.

After dinner, I did my homework and put all my laundry in a pile to take downstairs. Then I checked my e-mail, which I hadn't done in a week. I usually only got spam in my inbox because everyone I knew called my cell phone.

I was deleting the tenth mortgage offer in a long list of junk mail when I saw it: a message from Eli. I checked the date and time. He had sent it an hour earlier. The subject header read Thanks. My stomach did a little flip.

Hey, Kate—Just wanted to thank you again for the ride home. I owe you one. See you later. Eli.

I read the message five times, then called Lan and read it to her five times.

"What do you think?" I asked.

"I think he sent you a thank-you message," she said, yawning.

"But it could be more than that, right? I mean, he thanked me when he got out of the car. He didn't have to send an e-mail."

Lan didn't answer. I thought she was considering the possibility, but her breathing began to slow down.

"Lan?"

"Huh? Sorry, must have dozed off."

"I'm that boring?"

She laughed. "No. I was up late last night working on another paper. Nothing motivates me more than a deadline."

"Well, get some sleep. I'll talk to you tomorrow."

After we hung up I read the message one more time. It was probably nothing, I decided. He was just being polite.

I turned my attention to downloading the pictures I had taken at Tiffany's invitation ceremony. Overall, I was pleased with them. I liked crowd shots because they weren't posed. No one looked at the camera. No one even noticed it. Everyone wore their natural expressions. I could see some people smirking while others looked truly excited and filled with anticipation. My favorite picture out of the bunch was one with Tiffany herself. She was holding the bullhorn, her mouth half-open, surrounded by the camera crew and half the student body. She looked perfect, except for one flaw—her tiara had tipped to the side. It was like no matter how precisely she had planned her special moment, it just couldn't be perfect. There was something I liked about that idea.

After I finished saving my pictures I took my laundry downstairs, said good-night to my dad and got ready for bed. The stars on my ceiling glowed and I tried to remember which constellation was Gemini, then gave up and searched for Orion.

I couldn't sleep. I wondered what Eli saw in Reva. Was it her cool confidence? She seemed so much older to me, like she was a twenty-five-year-old woman trapped in a sixteen-year-old's body. Did Eli like her maturity? They had been together for over a year. Was it possible they would break up soon or would they stay together until graduation? It shouldn't have mattered to me, but it did.

I dreamed that night that I was in a dark tattoo parlor. Reva was there, holding a tattoo gun and smiling. "You shouldn't be here," she said, laughing.

"I want that one," I said, pointing to a picture on the wall. I couldn't really see it, but I knew I wanted it.

Reva shrugged. "Whatever."

I sat down in a chair and waited. Reva pushed the needle into my shoulder, but I didn't feel any pain. When she pulled away, I looked in a mirror. There, at the top of my arm, was a single gorilla.

"It's never coming off," Reva warned.

I stared at my arm. "I don't want it to."

8

RED STREAMERS HUNG FROM the gray cafeteria ceiling, draped in between metallic pink hearts. I took a few pictures as several freshmen boys tried to jump up and pull the dangling hearts down, but the boys were too short and didn't even come close. Some people applauded their efforts while others booed, attracting the attention of one of the vice principals. The boys scurried away before they could get in trouble.

It was Monday, and Valentine's Day was less than a week away. Lan and I were eating lunch with Eden Alder, who was trying to sort through a stack of "Heart Grams," her big fundraiser for the newspaper. She sold little heart-shaped ads, and people could write a few sentences to someone. The message would appear in a special section of the paper. Most of the messages were anonymous, but a lot of people bought them for their friends. Lan and I always got one for each other with a simple message, like "You Rock," or something.

"I just cannot believe how many ads people bought for Tiffany," Eden said as she flipped through a stack of paper slips, looking for mean or gross messages. There were always a few, and her job was to weed them out before the paper was published. She had missed an insult the year before, and Principal Carter had gone ballistic.

Lan rolled her eyes. "How many?"

"So far, twenty-seven. And I'm not done counting. We're going to have to add an extra page."

Eden had been invited to the party so she could write about it for the paper, but when she found out that her loyal assistant, Austin, didn't get an invitation, she angrily confronted Tiffany. Eden said that if Austin wasn't at the party, she wasn't coming and, if she wasn't there, Tiffany could forget about having a feature article in the *Cleary Chronicle*. Tiffany backed down, and Austin received his invitation the next day. I wished that I had the clout to do that so I could demand that Lan be invited. Of course, I still didn't know why I had been invited in the first place.

"Twenty-seven? Is that some kind of record?" I asked.

"I think so. Trent usually gets a dozen, and he's always had the most."

"What do the ads say?" Lan asked.

"They're stupid. 'You're the best,' 'You're so cool,' that kind of thing."

"So lies, basically," Lan muttered. Eden didn't seem to have heard her, but Eden was good at staying neutral, as long as it was a topic that didn't affect the paper.

I looked across the room at Trent's table and spotted Eli. Reva was sitting next to him, one hand running up and down his arm in a slow caress. I sighed. It didn't look like they had broken up, after all. I had selfishly hoped that their fight on Tuesday would be the end of them as a couple.

"Who are you looking at?" Lan asked.

"Nothing," I said. "I mean, no one."

Lan smiled. "Okay."

"Later," I whispered, shooting a glance at Eden. She seemed too immersed in her stack of Heart Grams to notice, though.

"I still have to turn in my Valentine's message," I said to Eden.

"No, I've got it."

I was confused. "I paid for it, but I haven't turned in the slip yet."

Eden looked up, a red pen poised in her hand. "The ad for Lan, right? I saw it this morning."

I frowned. "I haven't turned it in yet."

Eden shrugged. "I guess someone else bought her a Love Gram, then," she mumbled as she returned to reading her papers.

I looked at Lan. We usually knew ahead of time if someone was buying us an ad. Sometimes a group would go in and buy a message for someone to cheer them up, especially if one of our friends was immersed in the aftermath of a breakup, which happened a lot. I had a theory that guys purposely dumped their girlfriends just before Valentine's Day so they wouldn't have to buy them expensive chocolate or neon teddy bears or cheap, sparkly jewelry. A lot of couples seemed to fall apart around February 12, only to get back together a week later.

The lunch bell rang and we stood up and headed for the doors.

"Who do you think bought me a Love Gram?" Lan asked.

"Could be anybody," I replied, but I suspected that Brady was making his first move.

As we were squeezing ourselves out of the narrow cafeteria doorway, I felt a tap on my shoulder. Actually, it was more like a sharp poke, and at first I thought it was just part of the cattle mentality: someone from the back of the herd needed desperately to get to the front so they could use the bathroom before class started. I shifted to the side to let whoever it was get through before they were trampled or had an embarrassing accident.

"Ahem. Kate?"

I was out in the hallway now. Lan had already turned the corner on her way to fourth period English. It was still crowded, but at least I could no longer feel someone's breath on my neck. I turned around. Tiffany was standing there, causing a traffic jam just outside the cafeteria doorway. People maneuvered around her like ants trying to crawl around a rock. If it had been anyone else, the departing crowd would have shoved her aside with an annoyed grunt.

"Yes?" I wasn't sure if she was speaking to me, but she was just rooted there with Monica and Mallory close behind.

"First of all, I'm so glad that you can make it to my party," Tiffany began. I couldn't tell if she was being sarcastic or not. I glanced at Monica and Mallory. They weren't smirking or laughing, so I thought maybe Tiffany was being serious.

"And it's *so* nice of your dad to help out with security and all." Tiffany began to twirl a strand of her shiny auburn hair. I was aware that people were looking at us. They were probably wondering what Tiffany had to say to me that was so important. Was she uninviting me to the party?

"I mean, keeping the roads safe is a *really* important job." Tiffany gave me a wide-eyed look which I guess she thought made her look sincere. I knew she was trying to make a point, but I didn't get it yet.

"Right," I said. I tried to calculate how many minutes I had until the bell rang. Three, maybe.

"But maybe you could do me a little favor? You know, as a *friend?*"

I immediately understood two things: one, that Tiffany had invited me to her party knowing that she would be asking me for something in return; and two, that this would be my one chance to secure an invitation for Lan. I tried to stand a little taller.

"Maybe," I said, hoping I sounded bored and indifferent.

"Well, it's just that I'm sure the police department has *way* more important things to do than sit around by the side of the road waiting for speeding cars, right? I mean, there are real criminals out there."

"There's a maniac spray-painting every building in town," Mallory said. Monica was nodding like a bobblehead doll, although bobbleheads, I thought, somehow looked more intelligent.

"So maybe you could ask your dad to back off a little? I mean, my parents will be there, and we have our own security team, so it can't get *too* crazy, you know?"

I tried to appear naive yet serious. It's a difficult look to achieve because it involves furrowing your brow like you're thinking really hard and kind of biting your lower lip like you're uncertain about something important.

"I could probably do that," I said slowly.

Tiffany smiled. "I knew you'd be cool about it." She began to walk away. Monica and Mallory followed, their heels clicking against the tile floor.

"Of course, it might not be easy."

Tiffany stopped and turned around. Her smile was plastered

to her face, but there was something about the way her eyes were slanted that told me she was not pleased. She walked toward me, almost stomping in her black suede heels.

"Oh?"

"Yeah. I mean, my dad doesn't always listen to me. He may need some serious convincing."

"And how can I help you with that?" Tiffany asked. I could tell she was seething. Her smile was fading, and her right eye twitched.

"Well, Lan is really good at talking to him. If she was going to the party, I know she could help me convince him."

Something flickered across Tiffany's face. Monica's mouth hung open and Mallory was blinking like she had sand in her eye. It was like they were all in disbelief that lowly Kate Morgan had dared to ask for something from the mighty Tiffany Werner.

"I see," Tiffany said carefully. "Well, I'll tell you what. If you can get Lan to back off during history class, maybe I can find one last invitation."

"Good."

"It may be tough, though." Tiffany sighed. "My parents are being really strict about the number of people I can invite, and I'm already over the limit."

"Yeah, my parents are strict, too," I said. "Especially my dad."

I felt like we were in some sort of duel and I was struggling to keep the upper hand. She wanted something from me and I wanted something from her, but I got the sense that she was trying to get what she wanted without coming through for me.

"I guess we'll see," Tiffany said.

"I guess so."

She walked away and I waited a minute before heading to class. We were going in the same direction and I didn't want it to look like I was following her.

I was thrilled—maybe I had gotten Lan an invitation, after all. I knew Tiffany was just using me. Of course, I also knew there was no way Dad would back down from watching the roads near Tiffany's party. But Tiffany didn't know that.

I met Lan at her car after school. I had the day off from work, and we had made plans to go to the mall. Lan had the heat blasting as I got in and I put my hands directly in front of the vent to warm up.

"I think I know how to get you invited to the party," I told her as we sat at a red light. I described my encounter with Tiffany. "So all you have to do is not, you know, go after her during history class."

"Is that all?" Lan said sarcastically.

"What's wrong?"

"She basically said the price of admission to her party is to smile and keep my mouth shut?"

I squirmed in my seat. Lan was not as happy as I thought she'd be.

"I guess," I said. "I mean, it's just for a few weeks."

Lan made a left onto the main road. I could see Something's Brewing in the distance. It looked like there was quite a line of cars pulling into the parking lot.

"I can't do that, Kate," Lan was saying. "I appreciate what you're trying to do, but I'm not going to stop expressing my opinions just to make someone I detest look good."

"I thought you were just 'expressing your opinion' to tick her off. I didn't think it really meant something to you."

"Well, maybe that's why I started doing it, but I was talking to Brady the other day, and he said—"

"Wait. When were you talking to Brady?"

"Before class on Friday. Anyway, he said..."

We were almost to Something's Brewing. There were a ton of cars in the parking lot and a line all the way around the building. I knew Bonnie and Eli would have more work than they could handle by themselves. I wondered if I should just ask Lan to drop me off.

"...that he's not going, either. In fact, Brady thinks his whole group is going to boycott the thing. And I, for one, am glad. Tiffany has no power if we don't give it to her...."

That's when I saw it. The cars surrounding Something's Brewing were not waiting in line for drinks. They had been drawn there by something else entirely.

"Lan, pull over," I said. I was staring out the window and she looked over to see what had caught my attention.

"Oh, wow," she breathed.

She pulled the car over to the side of the street because there was no room left in the parking lot. Lan turned off the ignition and we sat there, looking at the side of one purple wall. Only, it wasn't really purple anymore. Painted across the wall, covering it from top to bottom, was a single, lifelike gorilla.

9

"Look, there's Trent and Brady," Lan said, pointing to a group gathered in the parking lot of Something's Brewing. The guys were leaned up against a car, talking. Lan turned off the ignition and reached for the door handle. "Let's go."

I wanted to see the gorilla painted on the building up close, but I also wanted to go inside. I saw Reva standing with the guys, hugging her arms to her chest in the cold.

"I think I'll just go inside and see Bonnie," I said. "I'll meet you out back in a few minutes."

We got out of the car. Lan headed for the crowd while I went around to the back door of Something's Brewing. I tried the handle but it was locked, which was unusual. Just as I was about to knock, it opened.

"Saw you coming," Eli explained, letting me in. He looked exhausted. His hair was flat, like he'd been wearing a hat all day, and his eyes seemed kind of dull.

"Is she really upset?" I asked him. Moving from the chilly outside air into the sweet-smelling warmth of Something's Brewing was a welcome change.

"Bonnie? No, she's not upset."

I found that hard to believe. Her business was her life, and now someone had defaced it. I was angry for her.

"Bonnie!" I called as I walked down the short hallway to the main room.

She turned around, a tall cup of coffee in each hand. Her apron was a little lopsided and her usually perfect hair was messy. She looked frazzled.

"Oh, Kate, I'm so glad you're here! It's been crazy. Could you make me two double espressos? Thank you, dear."

I rushed over to the espresso machine while Eli helped Bonnie. When I glanced out the window, I couldn't see an end to the trail of cars winding around the building.

"It's been like this for hours," Bonnie explained as she opened the cash register. "Some are here to look at the art-work, but nearly everyone who stops by is getting a drink." She laughed. "We've done more business in two hours than we have in the past two days."

I understood why increased business would make Bonnie happy, but I wondered how she felt about the gorilla splashed across the wall. Would she be angry after everyone left?

Eli and I worked like crazy for the next half hour. I forgot about Lan until I heard a knock at the back door. Eli ran to see who it was while Bonnie and I finished half a dozen cinnamon cappuccinos.

Lan walked in, but stood in the hallway so she wouldn't be in our way.

"One sec," I told Bonnie.

"Of course, dear. You've been such a help."

I apologized to Lan for making her wait. "I don't think I can go to the mall," I said, trying to prevent a thick curl of hair from falling into my face. "Bonnie needs all the help she can get." I searched my pockets for a rubber band. Lan reached into her purse and handed me two bobby pins.

"It's no problem," she said. "Actually, Brady and I thought we'd get something to eat. When do you think you'll be done? I can swing by and pick you up later."

I pushed a bobby pin through my hair. "No idea. It could be an hour or more." I wanted to ask her about Brady, but I didn't want it to be a rushed conversation.

"Kate, I can give you a ride," Eli hollered.

"You don't have a car," I hollered back. Eli handed a completed order to Bonnie and hurried over to me and Lan.

"I can use Brady's car. He lets me borrow it. He'll know where to hide the keys."

Lan smiled. "Great. I'll let him know. Brady and I will take my car."

"Tell him I'll bring it back tonight," Eli said. He turned to me. "I owe you one, remember?"

"Sounds like a plan," I said, but Eli was already back at Bonnie's side.

Lan nudged me. "Have fun," she whispered with a smile.

I returned to my post at the espresso machine and watched from the window as Lan and Brady went to her car. They were walking in step with one another, their heads close like they were sharing a secret.

I also caught a glimpse of Reva. She was still standing next to Trent, but she wasn't looking at him. She was looking directly at me, her arms folded across her chest, a look of pure hatred darkening her face. I quickly looked away, but I could still feel her staring at me. I shuddered. No one had looked at me like that before, and it gave me the creeps.

We worked at warp speed for the next hour. Eli was constantly running to the storeroom for more napkins or cups or lids, and we nearly ran out of caramel syrup, but things slowed down slightly after a while, and I began to relax. Reva was long gone, as was most of the high school crowd that had gathered outside Something's Brewing, but when a TV van pulled into the parking lot, I knew we needed to brace for another rush of customers.

Bonnie lit right up when she saw the news van. "Do I look okay?" she asked me. She fussed with her hair while I made sure her hand-knit sweater, which was the same shade of purple as the building, was free of lint. I wet a napkin and dabbed at a little spot of whipped cream on her sleeve.

"Perfect," I said.

Bonnie looked around. "I hate to leave you two when we're so busy."

Eli told her not to worry. "We've got it under control. Just get out there and start smiling."

"I'm giving you both a raise," she said as she rushed out the back.

I laughed. "I think we've earned it today."

A steady stream of customers poured through the parking lot for the rest of the day. Bonnie gave an interview to the local news in front of the gorilla mural. A cameraman came inside the building for a few minutes, but I was too busy to really pay attention to him. He stayed in the tiny hallway, and I doubted the footage would air on TV.

I called my dad to let him know I would be home late, and

he told me not to worry. "You mom's working, too," he explained. "So we'll eat late tonight." He knew about the graffiti, of course, and had already spoken with Bonnie. "She didn't seem to mind it," he said. "In fact, she didn't want to fill out a police report, but you know, it was procedure."

I told him we were swamped but that I had a ride home. I didn't tell him who my ride was, though, and I think he assumed it was Lan.

Something's Brewing stayed open an extra hour that day. The local news did a live feed at six, and minutes later the phone was ringing from all the people who had seen it, including my mom.

"You were on TV!" she exclaimed as soon as I picked up the wall phone.

"Oh, no," I said, immediately putting a hand to my hair. I knew it looked terrible.

"You looked fine," she reassured me. "When will you be home?"

"About an hour, I hope."

"See you then!"

I glanced at the clock. It was almost seven. We had served over a hundred customers in just three hours. I was spent, but Bonnie beamed with delight.

"That gorilla was more effective than any new sign I could have come up with," she said.

"You're really not mad?" I asked. The extra business was great, but it wouldn't last. Would Bonnie want to get rid of it once things went back to normal?

"Have you looked at it? It's quite something."

"I haven't had a chance," I admitted. It was already dark

outside. I would have to wait another day to really get a good look at the mural.

We cleaned up quickly and the three of us left together. Eli and I waved as Bonnie hopped into her silver minivan and took off, still smiling. The only car left in the lot was an old burgundy sedan.

"We call it 'the Beast,'" Eli joked. He opened the driver-side door and fished around under the seat, pulling out a handful of burger wrappers, half a CD and the car keys.

"I don't want to know what else is under there," I said as I got in, brushing crumbs from the passenger seat with my hand. The inside of the car smelled like cinnamon air freshener and wet socks.

Instead of leaving the parking lot of Something's Brewing, Eli turned the car around so it faced the side wall. "What are you doing?" I asked.

He just smiled. "Giving you a better look." He flipped on the headlights and suddenly, there it was: the gorilla.

I gasped. I had seen the same image on the school and at the tuxedo shop, but not like this—at night, illuminated so that there was nothing else to see except the perfect black paint.

I stared at it for a while, grateful that Eli wasn't talking. The gorilla was flawless. Better than flawless—the eyes had that liquid look to them, and the mouth seemed to curl faintly at one corner, as if it was caught just before a smile erupted on its face. I noticed something else, too—what looked like words in the lower-left corner, near one of the gorilla's feet.

"What does that say?" I asked Eli.

He leaned forward. "I don't see anything."

I pointed. "Right there. I can see words." I got out of the

car and knelt down by the wall. "Art lies," I read aloud. I turned around, but Eli was still in the car, so I got back in.

"It says 'Art lies.'"

"That's strange."

I wondered if the same two words had been painted on the other murals. "Can we stop at the bank?"

"Which one?" Eli asked, shifting the car into Reverse.

"The one I haven't seen yet," I replied. He understood, and soon we were headed toward the abandoned building.

We didn't talk much on the ride over. I glanced at the clock, knowing I had less than half an hour before I needed to be home. The bank wasn't far, though, and within minutes we were pulling into the empty parking lot. Eli drove around the building and parked in front of the mural, again using the headlights to light up the gorilla painted there.

"It's really something," I murmured.

"When money speaks, the truth is silent," Eli said, reading aloud the words painted above the gorilla's head.

"That sounds like a proverb or something," I said. "Like the artist was quoting someone."

I leaned forward in my seat so I could search for any words written into the gorilla's fur. I spotted them right away—the same words, painted in the same place near the feet: *Art Lies.* I pointed it out to Eli, who nodded. He seemed to be studying the painting just as closely as I was, as if it might hold other clues that we could find if we just stared hard enough.

"You know what's funny?" I said finally. The silence had started to become uncomfortable, and I wanted to break it.

"What's that?"

"My life is a lot like the bakery where my mom works."

"Packed with refined sugar?"

I laughed. "No. It's just that everything seems to come in waves." I explained how the store would get busy and hectic for an hour, then quiet and empty.

"Like right now, there's so much going on," I said. "Everything in my life feels frantic, like one thing on top of another. I guess I'm wondering when it will slow down again."

"Do you want it to slow down?" We were both still staring at the gorilla. It was so lifelike, I felt like it could really see us.

"No," I said after a moment. "I think I like it like this."

I sat back. Eli flicked off the headlights and we sat in the dark silence of Brady's car. I was about to comment on Lan and Brady going out to dinner together when Eli spoke up.

"Can I kiss you?" he asked softly.

It took me a second to register what he had just said. I turned to him, startled. I felt my heart beat faster as he looked at me. Even in the dark I could see his brown eyes and the soft smile on his face. I didn't say anything. Instead, I leaned closer to him. He put one arm against the small of my back, pulled me in and kissed me.

His mouth was warm and tasted like coffee and mint. Our kiss was slow and gentle and I felt like I was melting into him. My mind was racing. Here we were, kissing in Brady's car, parked at night behind the abandoned bank.

I pulled away abruptly.

"Are you okay?" Eli asked. "Did I do something wrong?"

"Kevin," I said. It just popped out.

Eli frowned. "You were thinking about that guy you dated last year? The one who dumped you?"

"Yes. I mean, no. Not exactly." I explained that Kevin and

I had once parked behind this same bank, quickly adding that nothing much had happened, and how he had broken up with me here, as well.

"So not the best place for our first kiss?" he asked. I was thrilled that he had referred to it as our first kiss, like there may be more in our near future, but the thought that had pulled me from him a moment earlier came crashing back to me.

"I didn't mean to say Kevin. I meant to say Reva."

Eli looked down, but I continued talking.

"Kevin started dating someone before he broke up with me," I explained. "That's what hurt—that he didn't have the decency to tell me it was over with us first. I don't understand what's going on with you and Reva, but if you haven't completely broken up with her, you need to before anything else can happen with us."

"She knows it's over." He looked me in the eyes. "We fight all the time. It's been over for a while."

"Have you *told* her that?"

Lan told me once that guys always think the relationship is over before girls do. She said guys will start making plans and moving forward while girls think the relationship can still be salvaged. What girls interpret as a rough patch, guys see as the end.

Eli looked out the window. "It's complicated."

"It always is." I sighed. "I really like you, Eli. I want to be with you. But you need to talk with Reva and end things completely before we can be together."

Part of me could not believe I was saying any of this. Reva hated me and here I was, trying to convince her boyfriend to do the right thing when all I really wanted was to kiss him again. Another part of me knew that if I wanted to be with Eli, to really have something with him, then we needed to start off right, without a lot of baggage or loose ends.

We were quiet for another moment. Eli looked at the dashboard clock, which was fast by a full hour, and turned the headlights back on.

"I'll talk to her tonight," he said. "I promise."

I squeezed his hand. He squeezed back, then pulled my hand toward his lips and kissed it lightly.

We were silent on the ride home. There didn't seem to be anything to say. But Eli held my hand the entire time, and when we pulled in front of my house, he didn't let go.

"Would it be okay if—"

I didn't let him finish. I leaned over, kissed him goodnight and hopped out of the car. I hoped he would drive straight to Reva's house. I knew it would be difficult, but he could end it immediately and we would deal with the aftermath together.

I stayed up late to watch the news with my parents that night, and sure enough, there was a three-second shot of me handing someone their coffee. Eli wasn't facing the camera, but I loved seeing him on TV, even if it was just his beautiful lean back. It was strange to have that moment captured on film. It was only an hour after that, I realized, that we were kissing in Brady's car.

Lan wasn't answering her phone, which probably meant the battery had died, so I gave up trying to call her and went to bed, excited that I had news to tell her and hoping that she had news to tell me.

I barely slept that night. I could still feel Eli's lips on mine as I gazed at the stars on my ceiling. The constellations had never seemed more clear to me.

10

I DIDN'T SEE ELI AT SCHOOL the next morning, which wasn't unusual, but I was hoping to catch a glimpse of him in the parking lot or the hallways or even near my locker. I lingered a little longer than I usually did before class, scanning the crowd for his face.

"You'll see him at lunch," Lan reminded me as we sat down at our desks for first period history.

I frowned. "I'll see Reva there, too."

I was already dreading the time—and I knew it was coming—when I would have to face Reva. Even if Eli left my name out of the breakup conversation, she would know soon enough that I was a factor. I remembered the hard stare she had given me the day before, and it made my stomach ache.

Mr. Gildea was taking attendance, which gave Lan and me a few minutes to chat.

"So what's going on with you and Brady?" I whispered.

Lan glanced over her shoulder at Brady's desk, but he wasn't there yet.

"Kate, he is so nice. I mean, he's not the kind of guy I'd usually go for, but I think—"

"Has anyone seen Mr. Barber this morning?" Mr. Gildea asked. People shook their heads. Mr. Gildea marked his attendance sheet and began class.

"I'll tell you later," Lan whispered. I nodded.

The morning debate was focused, of course, on the newest gorilla.

"It's one thing to tarnish a deserted building," Tiffany began, her voice full of confidence. With Brady absent and Lan supposedly backing off in return for an invitation, I think Tiffany felt she could run the discussion without anyone opposing her. "But the coffee shop is actually open. This vandal is costing a small business money. And it makes our town look bad."

I had wondered why Tiffany was so concerned with the graffiti. She wasn't the type to get upset about something that didn't directly concern her. But the graffiti, I realized, did affect her—or the way she would be perceived when the camera crew returned to town in just two weeks. She didn't want her half hour of televised fame to be marred by the murals, or worse, to be remembered forever as the girl who lived in the gorilla town.

I looked over at Lan, as did several others, to see what she was going to say in response. Without Brady to back her up, maybe she wouldn't say anything. Or maybe she had thought about it and she really did want to attend the party despite what it would cost her.

"But how does the owner feel about it?" asked someone from the back.

"Ask Kate. Doesn't she work there?"

People were now looking at me, which I hated. I self-consciously touched my hair, wishing I had a bobby pin. Mr. Gildea raised an eyebrow.

"Do you know how your boss feels about it, Kate?" he asked.

"Um, yes, actually." My voice sounded wobbly. I cleared my throat. "Bonnie—she's the owner—well, she likes it," I said. "It increased business yesterday. Plus, we had all that free publicity. She plans on keeping it up."

"So that ugly thing is going to be permanent?" Tiffany asked in disgust. "Are you kidding me?"

"Beauty is in the eye of the beholder," Mr. Gildea said mildly. "Let's take an informal poll. How many of you think the gorillas are ugly?"

Tiffany immediately raised her had. A few other people raised theirs, but a little more uncertainly. Slowly, other people raised their hands until it looked like nearly half the class was in agreement with Tiffany. Looking around, I realized that every single person with a hand up had been invited to her party—or wanted to be.

"Okay. So about half of you think the murals are ugly. Now how many of you think they're beautiful?"

A few hands, including Lan's, went up before Mr. Gildea could finish asking the question. I raised my hand, but a little more slowly. A few people didn't vote at all, but Mr. Gildea didn't push it.

"So we're about half and half," he said.

"I don't find them to be ugly or beautiful," said a girl in the back. "I think they're interesting."

"We have another opinion," Mr. Gildea said. "How many of you think that the gorillas are interesting?"

This time, most of the class raised their hands. Tiffany sighed loudly.

"Yes, Miss Werner?"

"Mr. Gildea, you're missing the point."

"And what point would that be?" He kept his voice calm, but I knew Tiffany was edging very close to the line with our teacher. The second he thought Tiffany was being outright disrespectful, he would call her on it.

"The point is, you can't tolerate crime just because some people think it's cute."

"I think the term used was 'interesting,' but you do have a point, Miss Werner."

Tiffany sat back, satisfied.

"However," Mr. Gildea continued, "I think the point our class has focused on for the past month is centered on whether or not this truly is a crime. Vandalism or art? I trust you remember the papers you wrote in January."

I had nearly forgotten about it. Mr. Gildea usually gave our graded assignments back within two weeks.

"There goes my B average," Lan muttered. I nodded. That paper had not been my best effort—not even close.

Mr. Gildea opened a manila folder. He walked down the aisles, handing us our essays.

"There's no grade on mine," someone said. I looked over my paper. There was not a single red mark on it anywhere. Mr. Gildea was known for passing back papers that were so heavily corrected they appeared to be bleeding.

"There is not a grade on any of them," he announced. I sighed in relief, but most of the class was annoyed.

"I worked hard on this!"

"I was up for hours typing it."

"This is so not fair."

Mr. Gildea held up one hand. "Let me explain. There is not a grade on it—yet."

There was more confused rumbling, which Mr. Gildea seemed to enjoy. "We have discussed this issue at length for over a month now," he said. "Many of you—" he looked directly at Tiffany "—have asked me what the point of the debate has been. The point, quite simply, was to get you to look at the issue from different perspectives."

He walked slowly back and forth in front of us with his hands behind his back, something he did when he was thinking. "I want to see if our class debate has changed the way you think about this topic. Your assignment is to reread your essay and decide whether or not it still reflects the way you feel about the definition of art."

Our homework was to read our own work? Easy, I thought.

"If your definition has not changed, simply add a sentence to the end of the paper saying so. If your definition has changed, you must explain how and why. I am giving you two weeks to complete the assignment. It will be worth a test grade." He wrote March 5 as the deadline on the board and began his history lecture for the day.

We all knew it was a devious scholastic scheme. When a teacher gives you two options, and one of those options is to basically do nothing, it's a trap. It was strange to me that he was giving us two full weeks to complete the revisions, when he had given us only one night to write the original draft. What was he trying to do besides confuse us completely?

I tried to focus on the Roman Civil War and take notes,

but there was too much to think about. I was counting the minutes until lunch. I just wanted to see Eli.

LAN WAS GIDDY. We'd barely had a chance to talk all day, but we'd been slipping each other notes in the hallway, which made me feel like we were in middle school again, but I didn't care. I was looking forward to lunch, when I could talk with Lan and finally see Eli.

I nearly ran to the cafeteria when the bell rang. I was the first one at our table, and I made sure that I picked a seat that had the best possible view of Eli's table across the room. Lan was next to arrive, and she began talking as fast as possible.

"So Brady and I hung out for hours," she said, almost breathless. "And he was so sweet."

I was listening to Lan, but I was also glancing over to my right every few seconds. Eli's table was nearly empty. Just a few guys sat there. No Eli and no Reva, either.

Ten minutes into the lunch period I realized that he wasn't coming. It was strange how Eli, Reva and Brady were all absent.

"Did Brady say he wouldn't be at school today?" I asked Lan. Something felt off.

She shook her head as she chewed on her sandwich. I barely had an appetite, but managed to eat some fries and half an apple before the bell rang. I saw Trent as I was heading toward English and I walked a little faster to catch up to him.

"Trent!"

"Hey, Kate," he said casually. He slowed down and zipped up his gray jacket. I was a little out of breath from trying to catch up to him—Trent had long legs and his normal pace of walking was like running to me.

"Do you know where Eli is today?"

Trent stopped in the middle of the hallway. "He's not here?"

"No. Neither is Brady. Or Reva, for that matter."

"Huh." Trent furrowed his brow. "I'll look into it," he said, and before I could ask him anything else, he turned around and walked to the doors leading to the student parking lot.

I didn't see Trent the rest of the afternoon. Lan gave me a ride to work after school, and as we pulled into the parking lot, I knew it would be another busy day. There was a line of cars, which was unusual for three in the afternoon.

"I'll call Brady as soon as I get home," Lan promised as I got out of the car.

"Let me know if you find out anything."

Bonnie was making drinks when I walked in, and an unfamiliar woman was manning the cash register.

"Kate, dear, this is Lila," Bonnie said. "She's my neighbor. She'll be helping out while Eli's gone. Would you make a chocolate praline cappuccino?"

"I've heard so much about you!" exclaimed Lila. She was plump and pretty, like Bonnie, and her bright silver hair was piled on top of her head in a loose bun. She smiled at me and I tried to smile back, but my mind was racing.

I grabbed a bottle of praline syrup from the shelf above the cappuccino machine and made the drink on autopilot. I was still stuck on Bonnie's words.

"Eli's gone? Where?"

Bonnie handed two drinks to Lila, who passed them through the window to a couple in an SUV.

"I'm not sure, exactly. He'll be back next week, though."

"Tell her about your idea, Bonnie," Lila said excitedly.

"It was Lila's idea, really." She paused. "Banana lattes."

Bonnie and Lila both looked at me, waiting for a response, but I was still trying to figure out a reason why Eli would miss a week of work. During the past two years he had been late maybe three times, and he rarely missed a full shift.

"Well?" Bonnie asked.

"Sounds good," I said.

Lila clapped her hands together. "It's going to be wonderful! We'll start giving out sample cups tomorrow."

There was still a line of cars at the window, and we quickly returned to preparing drinks. "Business has been steady all day," Bonnie told me as we worked side by side. "I don't know how much longer this will last, but maybe this new drink will help keep our momentum."

"Eli didn't say anything about where he was going? It's not like him to miss work."

Bonnie looked at me. "I'm sure he's fine, Kate. He called me this morning and told me that something had come up. He wasn't specific, but I know Eli. It must be important."

How important? I wondered. I hoped Lan had been able to get hold of Brady. Not knowing was driving me crazy. I tried to focus on work. We were busy, which usually made the hours go by faster, but I couldn't keep my mind off Eli, and everything dragged. I made a couple of mistakes with orders, which I never do, and flinched every time the phone rang.

Dad was late picking me up, so I used the time to take a few pictures of the gorilla before calling Lan from my cell phone while I waited in the parking lot.

"Find out anything?" I asked as soon as she picked up.

"Sort of," she said. "I called Brady. He couldn't talk long, he was in some sort of meeting."

"A meeting?"

"Something's going on, Kate. Something *big*. I don't know what, but it has something to do with Eli. Check your e-mail when you get home. Maybe he sent you a message."

Dad pulled into the parking lot and I said goodbye to Lan.

"How was your day?" Dad asked. He sounded cheerful.

"Fine."

"I've got some interesting news." I barely listened, instead staring out the window at passing cars, but then he said something that caught my attention.

"What did you say?" I asked.

"I said, we caught the gorilla guy last night. Well, the police in Henryetta, Oklahoma, did."

"Who is he?" I was trying to put together a timeline. Was it possible to drive from Cleary to Henryetta in the same day? Could one person do it by themselves?

"A college student. I guess he was driving across country, painting a gorilla in each of the towns where he stopped."

"And he came back to Cleary four times?" It didn't make sense.

"That's what we're trying to figure out. We think he had help, but he's claiming it was all him. A few of the businesses want to press charges, so I don't know why he would want to take the blame for all of it."

The first thing I did when I got home was check my e-mail and, sure enough, there was a message from Eli with the subject line Sorry.

Hey, Kate—

Wish I could talk to you in person, but this will have to do. I talked to Reva last night. Not good. I can't explain right now—and not like this—but I promise I'll tell you everything later. For now, it's probably best that we keep some distance between us. I'm really sorry. There's just a lot going on right now. It's like you were saying last night— chaos comes all at once. I'm hoping it will calm down soon, and then we'll talk, okay?

I don't know how many times I read Eli's message. It was vague except for one point—we couldn't be together. I wanted to reply, but didn't know what to say, so instead I forwarded the message to Lan. Five minutes later she called.

"What does it mean, exactly?" I asked her. I turned off the computer and retreated to my room. "Is Reva going nuts? Is she going to come after me?"

The image of Reva on the rampage was an unpleasant one. I could picture her storming down the hallway to confront me at my locker and stabbing me in the chest with one of her spiky-heeled shoes in a fit of rage.

"I don't know what it means, but the timing is strange," Lan said. "Did you hear they caught the graffiti artist in Oklahoma? And now Brady and Eli and Reva are skipping school and Trent is acting weird."

The same thought had occurred to me earlier on the drive home from work. "But how are they connected?"

"I don't know, but they are. Maybe they're planning some crazy road trip to meet this guy."

"Sounds like something Trent would do." I picked at a stray thread poking out of my comforter.

"And Brady," Lan said. "We had a whole conversation the other day about whoever it was doing this, and he was really, I don't know, *protective* of him."

"What do you mean?"

"I mean, he thinks this guy is a local hero. He doesn't want to see him get in trouble or go to jail or anything. I think he'd protest the arrest if he could."

"So what's going on with you and Brady now, anyway?" I asked, rolling over onto my back. "Are you a couple or what?"

"I wouldn't say that we're a couple," Lan said slowly. "I don't know if there is a word for what we are."

I decided it was time to tell Lan everything I knew, starting with my conversation with Eli and how Trent would never date a girl one of his friends liked. I said that Brady was definitely into her, and that in my humble opinion as her best friend, I thought they would be good together. When I was done talking she was quiet for a moment.

"You know where Brady took me to eat yesterday?" she asked.

"The mall food court?"

"No. He took me to a Vietnamese restaurant."

"Cleary has a Vietnamese restaurant?" I thought our tiny town was lucky to have a Denny's.

"No. We drove thirty miles to a little place Brady had looked up online. He wanted to make sure it would be something I liked."

"That's really sweet."

"It was. We stayed for three hours until they kicked us out. I got home late and my dad was furious—until he saw all the food we brought him."

"Brady met your dad?" This was big. Lan had never introduced a guy to her dad.

"He was so polite! Brady shook his hand and called him 'sir' and everything."

"Sounds like Brady's quite a guy."

"Yeah. Yeah, he is."

I knew it would work out for Lan and Brady, but I was worried about Eli and me. When would I see him again? Was the goodbye kiss we had shared just the night before our last?

"Kate? You still there?"

"Yeah. I'm just trying to figure out what's going on."

"You will," Lan said. "I'm sure this whole thing will get sorted out by tomorrow, and this time next week we'll be getting ready for a double date with Brady and Eli." She sighed contentedly and I knew she was smiling.

I hoped more than anything that Lan was right.

But deep down I feared she wasn't.

11

EDEN ALDER WALKED INTO THE cafeteria holding a warm stack of freshly printed newspapers. "The Valentine's Day special edition," she announced, dropping the stack onto our table. It made a soft thud and everyone immediately grabbed for a copy. People came over from other tables, too, and soon the stack was down to just a few folded issues.

It had been three days since I had last seen Eli. Trent and Brady were back at school, but Eli and Reva were not. Lan had tried to get Brady to open up about what was going on, but he told her he couldn't say anything. I guessed that it had something to do with the guy code they followed. All Brady said was that Eli's absence had nothing to do with me and that everything would be fine, "eventually."

"Eventually?" I said when Lan relayed the message. "So this could go on for another week? Or a month? Longer?"

I was completely frustrated. Lan tried to be sympathetic, but she was so happy with what was happening between her and Brady that it was hard for her to empathize with me.

Soon it was Valentine's Day, which arrived with the usual flurry of pink bears and delighted squeals. I sat at the lunch table, picking at a chicken Caesar salad, trying to ignore the heart-shaped boxes of chocolates being passed around. Brady had given Lan a pink-and-purple orchid in a white ceramic vase, and she carried it with her to every class. She even asked me to take a picture of it, which I did. It sat in the middle of the lunch table like a centerpiece.

"Ooh, look what Brady wrote to me," she said, pushing a newspaper in my direction. She pointed to one of the Heart Grams printed at the top of the page.

"Lan—Someone thinks about you every day. Someone just doesn't know what to say. Someone hopes you have a very happy Valentine's Day."

I smiled. "That's sweet."

I remembered how Brady had submitted the ad before Lan knew how he felt about her. I looked over at Trent's lunch table. Brady was gazing at Lan, and she waved at him, giggling. I wondered if she would begin sitting at his table, but I doubted it. Guys had a code, but so did girls, and one of the rules was that you always sat next to your best friend at lunch if at all possible. Lan knew I couldn't be near Reva, so she and Brady would be stuck staring across the cafeteria at one another, unless Brady decided to sit with us, which I didn't think would happen.

"This is just beautiful, Lan," said Eden. She was pointing to the orchid, which prompted Lan to gush about Brady, which caused me to tune her out for a while and leaf through the *Cleary Chronicle.*

Word of Tiffany's party must have spread to local businesses, because there were a lot more ads than usual, including one for the tuxedo rental place and two for dress shops. "Get ready to celebrate and SAVE 30%!" read one.

Eden had done her best to scatter the Heart Grams sent to Tiffany so they didn't overwhelm the rest of the paper, but they still dominated most of the pages. "You're SUPER!!!" they read, or "Tiff is SO AWESOME!!!" If Eden had charged by the exclamation points instead of the word count, she'd never have to worry about her budget again, I thought.

I scanned the pages, noting how most of the messages were so bland and generic they could have been written to anyone. But a small ad at the bottom of the last page caught my eye.

"Kate— Art lies, but I don't. I will make everything right."

I sucked in my breath. "Eden, when was this ad placed?" I asked, sliding the paper across the table. She glanced at it and shrugged.

"I've read three hundred of these things in the past seventy-two hours," she said with a sigh. "Oh, wait. That one came in on Monday, just before the deadline. That's why it's at the bottom of the page. Austin had to squeeze it in."

"Who dropped it off?"

"A freshman. I don't think it was from him, though." She rolled her eyes. "Probably running an errand for some senior."

I showed the message to Lan, who nodded. "See? It's going to work out," she said with an encouraging smile. I knew the message was from Eli, and it gave me a strange sense of calm. I looked over again at Trent's table. Most of the guys seated there were looking over the newspaper, but some of them were just talking. It was a crowded table, but to me it looked empty without Eli.

THE BANANA LATTES AT Something's Brewing proved to be a huge hit. Bonnie and Lila were thrilled with the newest addition to the menu and kept a special log of each one sold. "Thirteen today," Bonnie announced on Thursday. "I'm going to order a full case of banana syrup."

Lila found yellow T-shirts online with a big banana printed on the front, and she and Bonnie wore them every day. I could only smile and feign enthusiasm. Work just wasn't the same. It felt more like—work. Not even Bonnie's caramel coffee could cheer me up. She made me a banana latte, but I forgot about it and it sat on the counter all day, untouched.

I wasn't sure why people were flocking to the shop for such a strange drink, but maybe it was the appeal of something different. Coffee got boring after a while. The exotic lattes were a lot like the gorilla on the wall: unexpected and interesting.

While Bonnie and Lila chatted about new marketing strategies—I overheard talk of hiring someone to stand outside in a gorilla costume and prayed they wouldn't ask me to do it—I worked on my history essay for Mr. Gildea's class. The original draft didn't sound bad, but it wasn't strong. It began with the quote, "Life is short, art endures," and my main point was that the gorillas weren't really art because they could not endure, especially since half the town wanted them removed.

The three gorillas on the school wall were still there, though, even after repeated announcements that they would be sandblasted into oblivion. The official word was that Principal Carter needed to bring the work order before the school board, but I didn't think that was the case. Maybe he actually liked it.

I had examined the wall more closely after school, searching for *Art Lies,* and sure enough, the tag was there, near the foot of the third gorilla. I tried to think of a way to incorporate that two-word statement in my paper, but came up blank. In fact, I had no new or brilliant ideas for my essay. I decided to search the Web later for more art quotations, hoping there would be one that would inspire me.

The phone rang and Bonnie picked it up. "Hello, dear! We've missed you!" I perked up. Bonnie was either talking to Eli or one of her grandkids. I listened but tried not to look like I was listening by pretending to read the inventory list.

"Well, that's good news. I could definitely use you on Saturday."

Eli never worked on Saturdays. Was he changing his schedule?

"No, that's not a problem. Lila will be here. Take all the time you need."

It sounded as though Eli was not coming back the following week. I stood up and walked over to Bonnie. If she had Eli on the phone, I was going to talk to him and that was that. Bonnie looked at me.

"Is it Eli?" I whispered.

She nodded and I held out my hand, motioning for the receiver.

"One moment, dear, Kate wants to say hi."

"Eli?" I tried to keep my voice normal.

"Hi." He sounded surprised.

"Are you okay?" I asked, struggling to keep the worry out of my voice.

"Yeah, I'm okay."

"What's going on?" My stomach felt like cement.

"Um, I really can't say right now." I heard voices in the background, but I wasn't sure if there were people with him or if it was just noise from a TV.

"Can you e-mail me?"

He sighed. "Not really."

My fear that something was seriously wrong was washed away by a sudden wave of frustration. "Not really? What does that mean?"

"It's not a good time," he whispered.

"I don't understand."

"I can't talk now. I'll explain later. I'm sorry."

"So am I, Eli." I felt my voice break so I hung up the phone before he could say anything else. When I turned around, Bonnie and Lila were staring at me, their eyes wide.

"Are you all right, dear?" Bonnie asked gently.

I started to say something, but my words were choked out by my tears, which started unexpectedly and uncontrollably. I ran to the bathroom and tried to pull myself together. I cried for a while, then splashed cold water on my face. I looked in the mirror. My eyes were red and black mascara streaked my face. I was a mess, inside and out. I wiped at my face with a stiff paper towel, blew my nose and returned to work.

Lila was taking an order at the window and Bonnie was pouring steaming milk into a cup, but when they finished, they both turned their attention to me.

"Can we help you with anything?" Lila asked. Bonnie sat next to me and put one arm around my shoulder. I shook my head.

"I think I have to figure out this one on my own." I was touched that they seemed so genuinely concerned about me.

"Well, I think you need a little break," Bonnie said. "You've been working so hard lately. I want you to take the rest of your shift off, and don't worry about coming in tomorrow, either. Lila and I can handle it."

I nodded. I wanted to get away from the cramped space of Something's Brewing, at least for a little while.

"When is Eli coming back to work?" I asked.

Bonnie glanced at Lila. "Saturday will be his last day."

I didn't understand. "His last day until when?"

A car pulled up to the window and Lila turned away from us. I heard a man order two banana lattes.

"Eli is taking some time off," Bonnie said, her voice low. "He may not be coming back at all."

"What?" I felt the tears starting again, and I covered my face with my hands and tried to take deep breaths.

Bonnie rubbed my shoulder. "It's going to be fine, dear. This whole thing will blow over in no time."

I looked up. "What 'whole thing' will blow over?"

Bonnie seemed alarmed. "Oh, dear," she said. "I thought you already knew."

I felt a stab of panic. "Knew what? Bonnie, please tell me. I don't know what's going on and I haven't seen Eli in days. Is he okay?"

She patted my arm. "Yes, of course. He's fine. It's just…I don't know if I'm supposed to say anything."

Lila had finished with her customer and turned back to us. "Bonnie, for heaven's sake, look at the poor girl. Tell her."

I gave Lila a grateful smile. Bonnie cleared her throat. "Of course," she said. "But, Kate, please don't say anything to anyone."

I nodded.

"Eli isn't here," she began. "He's not in Cleary, I mean. He went with his parents to Oklahoma."

"Oklahoma? Why would he—"

I suddenly knew why, but I still needed to hear it said out loud. Bonnie cleared her throat again and looked me in the eye. "He's in Oklahoma because that's where his brother was arrested."

12

MY MOM WAS IN THE KITCHEN when I got home, walking from one end of the room to the other as she talked on the phone. She only paced like that when she was upset, but I could tell she was trying to keep her voice calm and controlled. I listened to her as I searched the fridge for a snack.

"Yes, I have that on the specification sheet you gave me," she said. "No, it's not in front of me at the moment. It's at work. This is my *home* number."

Mom sounded totally frustrated. I didn't know who she was talking to, but I knew that tone of voice, and whoever was on the end of the line had about two minutes to hang up or get yelled at. She was balling her fist so tightly her knuckles were turning white. Not a good sign.

There was nothing decent in the fridge, so I grabbed a box of crackers from the pantry and plopped down on the family room sofa. Mom came in a few minutes later and sat down next to me.

"Who was that on the phone?" I asked, my mouth half-full of cracker.

"A very rude customer," she replied, resting her head against the back of the sofa. She closed her eyes for a moment, then opened them and turned her head toward me. "You're home early."

"Yeah. Bonnie had her neighbor there. She's helping out and it wasn't too busy, so they said I could leave early."

"How did you get home?"

"Hitched a ride with some weirdo."

She bolted upright. "What?"

"Kidding. Lan picked me up."

Mom settled back into the sofa and closed her eyes. "She just dropped you off and left?" Usually Lan stayed for dinner or hung out or something.

"She was on her way to see her new boyfriend."

"That's nice," Mom murmured. She was falling asleep, so I took my crackers and went to my room for a while.

After the revelation that Eli's older brother Ben was the tagger behind half a dozen gorilla murals in several different states, I actually began to calm down. Finally, I had some kind of answer. I remembered that when the school was tagged in January, Ben had been in town. I wasn't sure how he had managed to create the other murals in Cleary, but it didn't seem to matter. What mattered was that Eli was in another state with his parents, which meant he was probably nowhere near Reva, one of my main concerns. I didn't know where Reva was, and I didn't care—I just didn't want her curled up next to my future boyfriend, tracing those razor-sharp nails of hers up and down his back.

I tried to block the image from my mind and went to research my history paper. Were we supposed to define art or support our position on the gorillas? Both, I guessed. I perused pages on art quotations and famous artists and European museums, but nothing inspired me. It occurred to me that I was trying to find someone or something else to answer a question that I needed to work out on my own. Mr. Gildea was smart to have given us two weeks to complete the essay. I wished he would have given us two months.

I gave up after an hour. Dad came home and we made dinner, careful not to wake Mom.

"She's had a lot on her plate lately, so to speak," Dad explained as he unwrapped a frozen pizza.

"I know the feeling," I said.

PARTIES SHOULD, BY DEFINITION, bring people together to celebrate. Tiffany's birthday bash, now less than two weeks away, was having the opposite effect on the students of Cleary High School. In fact, it would not be much of a stretch to say that "the social event of the year" had incited a small war.

The first battle began when Mallory discovered that one of the senior cheerleaders had purchased the exact same red silk dress as her.

"Take it back," she demanded. It was after lunch on Tuesday, and Mallory's high-pitched screeching attracted a small crowd in the hallway.

"I already cut the tags off," the cheerleader protested. She was surrounded by half the squad, all of them standing with their hands on their hips as if frozen in a choreographed dance move.

"I don't care! Take it back!" Mallory was close to tears. Monica took off in search of Tiffany.

"*You* take it back!" yelled the cheerleader. I was watching the scene from the back of the crowd. It was amazing to watch two normally composed girls transform into enraged toddlers before my eyes. It was like they were fighting over a doll.

The shouting got louder, the crowd got quieter, and soon two vice principals and a security guard arrived to break things up. Guy fights usually ended with punches thrown, but girl fights always ended with blood on the tile and chunks of hair strewn across the hallway, and the vice principals knew that better than anyone. I didn't think they had to worry, though— neither girl wanted to endure the trauma of unsightly bruises or challenging hair issues before the big night.

By the end of the day, Tiffany had decided that the cheerleader could still attend the party if she wore a cropped jacket and promised to stay away from Mallory the entire night. It was a compromise—not a good one, but it would work.

The incident reminded me that I had yet to shop for my own dress. Lan had been prodding me to get one, but I was waiting for her to receive an invitation.

"We'll go dress shopping together," I told her.

Lan nodded but said nothing.

Mallory's dress disaster was not the only conflict Tiffany had to contend with. The prom committee, which consisted of several popular seniors, was not happy with the timing of the party (only a month before prom), the theme of the party (too similar to prom, which was going to feature nearly the same shade of blue tablecloths) or the location of the party (they had also reserved the country club—six months in advance).

Ticket sales were way down. Most of the senior class would be at the party and had already announced that they would not be buying a second dress or renting another tux. The general feeling was that a free, exclusive party was much better than an expensive dance that anyone could attend. There was also the television coverage to consider. It looked like Cleary's prom was going to be canceled.

"It's not my fault," Tiffany announced to anyone who would listen. "People want quality, not tacky tradition."

She definitely had her supporters, but Tiffany was beginning to lose the admiration of half the senior class, most of the cheerleaders and all of the freshmen. Not that she cared, as she pointed out on an hourly basis. They were all just jealous, in her opinion. Still, she wasn't holding her head as high, and there were a few times in class when I glanced over and saw her staring into space, a blank look on her face. I wondered if she was realizing that her dream party was transforming into a nightmare. I felt a twinge of sympathy for her at those times, but it wouldn't last. Tiffany would always do something that made me want to strangle her, like pull out car catalogs and wonder out loud which high-priced luxury vehicle her dad was going to surprise her with.

"If it's not a convertible, I'll die," she announced before class one day. "I mean, what's the point of having a Beemer if you can't put the top down?"

Sometimes people would nod in fake understanding, but her spoiled-girl soliloquies were beginning to wear thin.

Lan hadn't mentioned the party in over a week, and I questioned if she still wanted to go. Once, as I helped her sort through tiny pink beads for an orchid pin she was making, I pondered the party's theme.

"Do you think it will be a kind of 'diamonds are a girl's best friend' motif?" I asked. "Because that's what I heard. Diamonds and pearls, that kind of thing."

"Pass me a few clear ones," Lan said, nodding toward a box of beads.

She hadn't been speaking up as much in class, but Lan still hadn't received an invitation. I wanted to approach Tiffany about it, but she was always surrounded by a small flock of fans. I decided to wait a few more days. If Lan decided she didn't want to go, that would be fine. I wanted her to have an invitation so that she at least had a choice. It wasn't that long ago, I realized, that her choice would have been clear. Now, I wasn't so sure.

Lan wasn't the only person causing me confusion. I was still waiting to hear from Eli. It had been eight days since I'd seen him, but it felt like eight weeks. I searched for him in the crowded hallways at school, my heart quickening any time I caught a glimpse of someone with his same shade of chestnut-brown hair. After school I checked my e-mail, hoping for a message, no matter how brief. And when the phone rang and the caller ID showed Unknown Number I always answered it, only to feel disappointed when it was the inevitable telemarketer.

My concern that Eli was okay had morphed into worry that he was simply avoiding me. Maybe he had reconsidered and decided our first kiss was an only kiss. Maybe Reva had found a way to win him back. Maybe he had spent the past week realizing that he didn't like me as much as he had. I came up with a new "maybe" every day, but they all boiled down to one depressing thought: maybe Eli and I were over before we ever began.

13

MAYBE IT WAS UNDERSTANDABLE that Tiffany Werner was not in a good mood on Thursday morning. Her party was only nine days away and judging by the heavy bags beneath her eyes she had not been sleeping well. More people seemed angry with her than happy for her, and Nothing Serious, the band scheduled to perform, was trying to back out of the deal. Three good reasons why anyone would be having a bad day. But there was no excuse good enough to justify what happened in history class that morning, and afterward, most people thought Tiffany had been lucky to make it out of the room alive.

It began like any other class day: Mr. Gildea took attendance while everyone chatted, then he collected homework and reminded us about our essay, which we had less than a week to finish. There were a lot of questions about the paper. Did we need to include historical references? How many pages? Was there a word count requirement? Everyone seemed anxious about it.

"I'm simply looking for strong support and evidence of critical thinking," he said with a bemused smile. "No page requirements, no word limit. It's done when you think it's done."

"But we should definitely mention the gorillas?" Lan asked.

That's when Tiffany began to unravel. Maybe she had been close to losing it all morning, but when she heard Lan say *gorilla* something snapped.

"That's it!" she screamed. And I mean screamed, like cover-your-ears-because-it-hurts screamed. She stood up, her hands visibly shaking. "I do not want to hear that word," she growled, her voice deadly.

I was looking from Tiffany, whom I half expected to start foaming at the mouth, to Mr. Gildea, who looked incredulous. I'd never seen him like that, like he had no idea what to do.

"Does everyone understand me?" she demanded, her voice starting to creep back up into screaming range. "I. Do. Not. Want. To. Hear. That. Word."

"Miss Werner, have a seat, please," Mr. Gildea said. His voice was gentle, like he was coaxing an angry dog. He hadn't moved from behind his lectern. I thought he was honestly afraid that she might bite him if he got too close.

Tiffany was glaring at everyone as if daring them to argue with her. When she made eye contact with Lan, she pointed a single shaking finger. "Don't say it, Lan. You're the worst one. Every time we discuss anything you have to bring it up and I'm sick of it! So just shut up, Lan! Shut! Up!" She stomped her foot so hard I thought the heel of her shoe was going to break in half.

Now the class was looking from Tiffany, who was still standing at the back of the class, to Lan, who was sitting at her desk, her cheeks burning pink.

"Do not speak to me that way," Lan said slowly. She kept her voice subdued, but anyone could see that she was fuming.

Tiffany went berserk. "I will speak to you any way I please!" she screamed. "And if you don't like it, you can go right on back to the rice—"

That's when Mr. Gildea lost it. "Miss Werner, sit down now!" he roared, drowning out Tiffany's words. It was the loudest I had ever heard a teacher shout. The glass on the door trembled a little, and everyone froze, mouths open. I don't think anyone even blinked. Mr. Gildea's face was a shade of purple I had never seen before, and Tiffany looked as if she had been slapped. She made a little choking sound before bursting into tears and running from the room.

An eerie silence settled over the class. We could hear Tiffany sobbing as she ran down the hallway. Doors opened and we heard teachers talking in the hallway, asking what was going on. There was a light knock at the door.

"Andrew?" It was the freshman history teacher from across the hall. "Everything all right in there?"

Mr. Gildea, still looking a little purple, opened the door and stepped out into the hallway. We all strained to hear what he was saying, but he was whispering. I reached across my desk for Lan's hand, and when she looked at me I could see that her initial rage had been replaced by a soft kind of sadness. Brady came over and knelt on the floor by her desk, asking her if she was okay. Lan nodded but didn't say anything.

The class began to whisper, and the whispers grew louder and louder until Mr. Gildea returned a few minutes later, at which point everyone automatically stopped talking and waited for him to say something. Instead of addressing us, though, he simply collected his papers and left the room. A nervous-looking sub came in a minute later and asked us to please study quietly.

LAN SPENT HER LUNCH PERIOD in the office with Mr. Gildea and Principal Carter, who had called her in to discuss "racial sensitivity." Tiffany had already left for the day. Her mother picked her up, and the rumor was that she wouldn't be back for a while. The other rumor was that she was going to check into a hospital for exhaustion.

I ate lunch with Eden and the rest of the newspaper staff. Everyone was buzzing about Tiffany's nuclear meltdown.

"I heard she tried to bite Mr. Gildea."

"She threatened to kill the whole class."

"They found a knife in her purse."

None of it was true, and I was about to clear a few things up when someone approached the lunch table.

"Kate."

I looked up at the sound of my name. It was Reva. She was dressed in black jeans and a black top and her nails were painted black. I panicked. Was she going to attack me here? Would she slit my throat with those deadly nails in front of a hundred witnesses? I saw Brady get up from his table across the room and walk swiftly over to stand behind Reva. It was bad, I thought, if Brady felt like he needed to hang around.

"Hi, Reva." I tried to sound neutral, but my voice came out like a strangled squeak.

"I wanted to let you know that Eli will be back at school tomorrow." Her eyes never left mine. It was like she was trying to see through me.

"Oh. Well, that's…great."

Reva continued to stand there. Was I supposed to say something else? Had Eli asked Reva to talk to me? Maybe it was a trap—she would remain silent until I confessed to stealing her boyfriend. The entire lunch table was silent. I hadn't told anyone else about me and Eli, but they knew something was off. Reva never spoke to me.

"We broke up," she said. Her voice was flat.

"I'm...I'm sorry to hear that."

"I'm sure you are."

Before I could respond, she turned and left the cafeteria. Brady looked at me, shrugged and returned to his table.

"That was weird," Eden remarked.

"Why is she telling you about Eli?" someone else asked.

"No idea," I said. "I have absolutely no idea what that was about."

Only one thing mattered to me in that moment, though— Eli was returning to school. I didn't know what it would be like to see him again, or what I would say to him, but he had promised to make things right. It was a promise I hoped he would keep.

I MET UP WITH LAN AFTER SCHOOL. I didn't have to work, so she was coming over to my house. I wanted to make sure she was okay after everything that had happened. She was quiet as we walked to her car, but I knew she would open up once we were in my room.

We had just made it to the parking lot when I noticed Monica and Mallory. They were parked just a few spaces down.

"One sec," I told Lan.

I approached Monica because she was the closest. She was already in her car, so I tapped on the glass and she rolled down the window.

"What do you want?" She was clearly annoyed.

"I need you to give Tiffany a message from me," I said as

loudly as possible. The parking lot was half-full of students, and I wanted them all to hear what I had to say.

"Tell Tiffany that I won't be at her party," I said. "I prefer to spend my time with people who actually possess a shred of class."

Everyone heard me and a few people chuckled. I began to walk away, even though Monica was hollering at me.

"You were going to be uninvited, anyway!" she yelled. "But don't worry, your mom can tell you all about how great it was. Maybe she'll take a few pictures for you, too."

I kept walking and pretended I hadn't heard.

"What did she say about your mom?" Lan asked.

"She said my mom would be at the party." Things started to make sense all at once: how Mom was so stressed with work and was coming home late every night, how she was mad at her boss and had a customer calling her at home—it was all related to Tiffany.

"Can we make a quick stop before we go to my house?" I asked Lan. She nodded.

Fifteen minutes later we pulled in front of Cleary Confections. Inside, the scent of warm bread filled the air. It was one of the slow periods. Mom's assistant, Bud, was wiping down the little café tables while easy listening music played softly from a tiny boom box behind the counter.

"Hey, Kate. Your mom's in the back." Bud tossed the rag he had been using over his shoulder. "I hope you're bringing her good news," he said quietly. "She's having a real bad week."

"What's going on?" Lan asked, her eyes darting toward the back.

"We're overbooked big-time. The boss took on way too

much. Now he's leaving for vacation and we're stuck with some huge orders."

I turned to Lan. "This might not be the best time," I said. "We can ask her later." Lan nodded. Mom was rarely in a bad mood, but when she was—watch out. Hell hath no fury like a stressed-out woman in an overheated kitchen.

"Bud! I need more buttercream and I need it now!"

Bud winced. "All week," he whispered to us. "It's been like this all week."

Before Lan and I could slip out of the store unnoticed, Mom walked through the swinging doors.

"Kate! What are you doing here?"

"Hi, Mrs. Morgan," Lan said.

"Hello, Lan." Mom gave her a weak smile and sat down at one of the café tables. She was a mess. Her hair was pulled into a sloppy ponytail, she wasn't wearing any makeup and her apron was crooked. Bud brought her a cup of coffee before heading to the back room.

"We're not staying," I said. "I mean, we can talk later."

"No, no. You're here. Sit. I need a break, anyway."

It felt like the worst time to ask her about the party, but I thought it might be one of my only chances to do so.

"So are you making Tiffany Werner's birthday cake?" I asked.

Mom sighed. "Yes, I am. Unfortunately." She shook her head. "I guess they had some fancy baker up in North Carolina all set to do it, but he backed out at the last minute. They offered Sam a huge sum of money." She stirred her coffee. "It's a total disaster. Bigger than a wedding cake, and it has to be hand delivered."

"Oh."

Mom stopped stirring her coffee. "That's the party you're going to, right? Don't worry, I'll be in the kitchen the entire time. You won't see me."

"That's not it," I said. I explained what had happened in school earlier. Lan added to it and, when we were through, Mom shook her head.

"I wish I didn't have to do this, girls, but it's not something I can get out of." She reached across the table and squeezed Lan's hand. "I'm sorry, dear. No one has the right to make you feel inferior. Ever."

Bud came out of the back room. "We need more blue," he said.

Mom sighed and got up. "We've made fifteen different batches of blue icing, and not one has been the right shade." She glanced at the clock. "Mrs. Werner is coming by soon. I need to get ready."

She gave both Lan and me a quick hug. "Tell Dad I'll probably be late again."

Once we got to my house, Lan's quiet unhappiness became a simmering rage. "I wish there was something we could do to sabotage this party," she said. We were in my room devouring a bag of chocolate cookies. In my opinion, misery loved not only company, but calories, as well.

"I thought about that," I admitted as I reached into the bag. "I don't know, though. Tiffany's doing a pretty good job of ruining this thing on her own."

Lan examined her cookie thoughtfully. "Still, there's got to be something we could do. Not awful," she added quickly. "But something to throw it off. Something to make it not so perfect."

"You're not going to do something crazy, are you?"

"No, of course not. It was just a thought."

"You sure?" It wasn't like her to back down so quickly.

Lan stood up and brushed crumbs off her jeans. "I'm sure."

I wanted to believe her, but something was different about Lan. Tiffany had crossed a line, and I was concerned that Lan was about to cross one in return. She was up to something. I hoped that whatever it was, she would tell me so I could talk her out of it. I wanted to see Tiffany topple from her pedestal just as much as Lan did, but I didn't think it would be possible to do anything to her at the party. A private security team would be monitoring the area and a half-dozen police cars would be stationed less than a mile away. If Lan got caught, she could be thrown into the back of a squad car with half the school and a camera crew watching.

I looked at my best friend. She was miserable. Maybe she was going to do something extreme, but if it made her feel better, I wasn't going to let her do it alone.

"If you need help, count me in," I said.

She smiled. "Thanks. I'm not going to do anything, though. You're right, Kate. Tiffany will ruin this thing on her own."

I was relieved that she wasn't going to try something that could get her into trouble, and even more relieved that I wouldn't have to get in trouble with her. I had meant what I said—I would stand by her no matter what—but the fear of public humiliation was nearly enough to make me want to back out of that promise. The party was now only a week away, and I wanted more than anything for it to be over so we could move on as if it had never happened.

14

HE WAS BACK.

I caught a glimpse of Eli shortly before first period on Friday. I stepped off the bus just as he was walking into the building, his backpack slung over his shoulder. I wanted to shout his name, but I didn't think he would hear me, and besides, I wasn't sure what I wanted to say to him. The last time we'd spoken I'd hung up on him, which was probably not the best way to have left things.

Once I was inside, I searched the hallways for Eli but didn't see him. There was a surprise waiting for me in my locker, though. He had written a brief note to me on a scrap of paper and slipped it through the grate.

"Hope we can talk later. I'll stop by SB around four. See you then?"

I smiled. Finally we would have the chance to talk. I nearly skipped to history class.

The rest of my morning was great. Tiffany wasn't in school, people were in Friday mode and my classes sailed by. I looked forward to lunch, when I could sit with Lan and glance over at Eli's table and see him. I wondered if Reva would still sit there now that she and Eli had broken up. I hoped not, but if she did, maybe she would sit at the far end of the table instead of right next to him. There had been times when she sat so close to him that it appeared she was sitting in his lap.

"Do you see him?" I asked Lan. She looked around, spotted Brady and gave a little wave.

"He's so sweet." She sighed. "He burned a CD for me last night. I can't wait to listen to it."

"Do you see Eli?" I was getting impatient. I wanted Lan to look for me. She had an excuse to stare at his table and I didn't. Not yet, anyway.

"I see Trent. And that guy who's always getting busted for skateboarding in the hallway. There's that other guy they hang out with, the one with the nose ring. What does he do when he has a cold?"

I let Lan ramble while I ate my lunch. "I know that guy's name but I can't remember it," she was saying. "I think it starts with an *A*. Adam? Aaron? Oh."

Her *oh* was like a rock dropping. It seemed to land with a thud and she abruptly stopped talking.

"What is it?" I asked.

"Nothing," she said brightly. A little too brightly, I thought. She turned toward me and I knew she was trying to block my view of Eli's table.

"Seriously, what's going on?"

I peered over her shoulder. I didn't see Eli right away, but I saw Reva standing at the very end of the table, partially blocked by some of the guys. She was dressed in skintight leather pants and a red shirt that sparkled when she moved. And she was definitely moving. As the nose-pierced guy got up to throw something away, I could see that Reva was standing behind Eli's chair, slowly rubbing his shoulders. He barely seemed to notice. He was talking to Trent across the table like it was the most natural thing in the world to have a girl giving him a lunchtime massage. Before I could look away, Reva leaned down and licked his ear.

"She said they broke up," I whispered to Lan. I felt like I was going to start crying, and I did not want to expose my emotions in the cafeteria.

"They did," Lan whispered back.

"Doesn't look like it."

My stomach hurt. It was like I had been punched, and I was suddenly sure that my lunch was not going to stay down. I pushed my chair back and hurried out of the noisy cafeteria to the bathroom. Once there, I found an empty stall and locked myself in until the bell rang. I leaned my head against the door and listened to the rumble of the crowd leaving the cafeteria. I wanted to cry, but I knew if I did I wouldn't be able to stop, so I took a few deep breaths and waited until it was quiet and I was sure that most people were gone. Then I washed my hands, checked my hair in the mirror and left the bathroom.

"Hey, Kate."

I spun around in the hallway, my heart beating fast. Eli was standing there, grinning. I couldn't believe that he was smiling at me like nothing was wrong when I had just seen his supposed ex-girlfriend running her hands all over his body. This time, I couldn't help it. I began to cry. Eli's smile slipped from his face and he rushed over to me.

"Are you okay? What's wrong?" He guided me to the nearest stairwell, which was deserted.

"I saw you." I was trying hard to stop crying. I didn't have a tissue in my pocket and my nose was running and there was nothing I could do about it.

"You saw me where?" he asked. I couldn't believe he was acting so naive.

"I saw you at lunch. With her."

"Oh."

I was sniffling. "Well?"

He ran a hand through his dark hair. "I didn't think you could see us."

I must have looked like I wanted to push him down the stairs because he started talking really fast. "What I mean is, yes, Reva and I have broken up. Officially. We're done. Really, we are. It's just…"

"Complicated?" I asked bitterly.

He looked hurt. He reached for my hand but I pulled away.

"Kate, I'm sorry. It really is nuts. She knows we're finished, but she's not letting go, exactly. And I can't upset her right now."

"But you can upset me?"

He reached for my hand again. This time, I let him take it.

"It's just going to take a little time, that's all." He was rubbing my arm and it felt nice. I closed my eyes. "This is going to be settled soon. Until then, I'm just trying to be nice."

I opened my eyes. "Does that mean you have to let her touch you?"

"No. I'm sorry about that. That shouldn't have happened."

I changed the subject. "How's your brother?"

Eli stopped stroking my arm. "Ben is fine." His voice was clipped. I had obviously said the wrong thing. Eli was looking away from me, at the empty stairwell.

"You okay?"

"Yeah, it's fine. I mean, I'm fine."

"You don't sound fine." I tried to say this as gently as possible. Eli shrugged. "Tired, I guess."

I wanted to say something reassuring. I wanted him to open up. I wanted to spend the rest of the day in that stairwell with him. We heard someone coming and both of us looked toward the steps. A teacher was walking our way, a cup of coffee in one hand, a stack of papers in the other.

"Where are you two supposed to be?" she demanded.

"Sorry," Eli mumbled.

"Get to class, both of you. Now."

We didn't argue. I turned and headed back to my locker. Eli went up the stairs. I didn't see him at all the rest of the day. I hoped he would still stop by Something's Brewing at four, but he didn't. I waited inside with Bonnie and Lila, helping out for an hour before I gave up on him coming.

I tried not to take it personally. We'd had a chance to talk, at least. He just hadn't said anything I wanted to hear.

THEY ARRIVED THE FOLLOWING Monday. When school ended, they were waiting for us in the parking lot: three red vans and a ton of wires spread across the pavement. I recognized one of the cameramen from Tiffany's invitation ceremony.

"Let the madness begin," I said to Lan.

Tiffany had been back at school that day, looking happy and refreshed. She was dressed casually in jeans and a white T-shirt, but it was a carefully choreographed kind of casual. Her silver jewelry glittered, her high-heeled boots clicked against the floor. She was back, and she was in control.

No one mentioned her history class breakdown. The official rumor was that she had gone to a spa for the weekend. Her skin did look good, I thought. She made a point to smile and say hi to Lan in front of Mr. Gildea, but her *apology,* if you could call it that, was flimsy.

"Sorry I freaked out last week," she said.

Lan just looked at her.

"I've been under a ton of stress," Tiffany explained. When it became obvious that Lan was not going to reply, Tiffany gave up. "I like your pin," she said, pointing to the pink orchid fastened to Lan's jacket. Tiffany then went to her desk, satisfied that all was right in the world. I resisted the urge to stick out my foot and trip her.

The student body had decided to forgive Tiffany for her transgressions. I think the sight of the camera crew helped. It was really happening, and people were getting excited. Even the cheerleaders were smiling. The camera crew set up their equipment and Principal Carter let them inside the school entrance on Tuesday to take a few shots and interview some of Tiffany's friends.

"She's just so…classy," I overheard one girl say. She looked into the camera with earnest eyes. "And we're all so excited about this party. It's going to be the biggest thing this town has ever seen."

I continued to see Eli in the hallways and at lunch. He always smiled or nodded to acknowledge me, and sometimes I found brief notes stuffed inside my locker but nothing too personal. Reva still sat beside him at lunch, but she kept her hands off him. I hated the distance between us, but I didn't feel like there was a lot I could do about it. Eli had to make the first move. And when he did, well, I wasn't going to embrace him with completely open arms. If he truly wanted to be with me, he had a lot of explaining to do. I didn't want to play games with him, but I also felt like he had kept me in the dark for too long.

Work was busy yet felt slow. Lila chatted nonstop and the customers kept coming back for banana lattes and things seemed normal in a way, but different in another way. It was like everything around me had stayed the same but I had undergone a silent, subtle change. I hadn't realized how much Eli had affected my everyday life until he was no longer a significant part of it.

The MTV vans could be seen all around town. Sometimes they drove next to whatever car Tiffany was riding in. They were mainly at her house, I heard, and she took Thursday off from school to fine-tune party details and only came to school Friday for the first three periods. She was in her element. I'd always suspected that Tiffany was one of those people who lived their lives as if a camera crew was always present, that she believed she had a secret hidden audience observing her every move. But now the audience was very real.

Lan and I made plans to crash at my house on Saturday, the day of the party. I rented a stack of DVDs and stocked up on energy drinks so we could stay awake all night, but at lunch on Friday she told me there was a slight change of plans.

"Nothing major," she said. "I just won't be over until a little later."

"How much later?" I asked. Reva had just laughed so loud that people were looking in her direction, and it was taking everything in me not to steal a peek at her table.

"Probably around nine. Brady wants to go out for bite to eat. He'll drop me off."

I wondered if Brady and Lan were going to try to sabotage Tiffany's party. I knew Brady would help her. He had become completely devoted to Lan over the past couple of weeks. I also understood that if Lan didn't want me to know about what was going on, there was probably a good reason. I was the daughter of the police chief and she was most likely protecting me from getting into trouble. I wanted to be a part of whatever it was she was planning, but I also did not want to go near Tiffany's celebration. It's one thing to be invited and then choose not to go. It's something else entirely to be un-invited. I wanted to pretend none of it was even happening. In just a few days it would be nothing but a faint memory, I thought. Somebody else's memory.

Reva laughed loudly again, and I shot a quick glance across the room. Trent was standing on his chair, doing some kind of weird dance. The rumor was that he was going to the party with a couple of friends. They had bought matching pink tuxedos at a thrift shop, and they were going all out: top hats, canes and fake mustaches. Tiffany's dramatic entrance was in danger of being overshadowed. She would need to have bald eagles carry her through a ring of fire to compete with Trent.

I was relieved when the final bell rang and school ended. I was looking forward to a quiet weekend with my best friend and forgetting about all the party craziness. I found a note crammed in my locker grate as I left school.

"Hey— Things are better. Let's do something on Sunday."

I smiled and put the note in my pocket. Maybe things could be normal again, after all.

MY DAD HAD BEEN WORKING with the Henryetta police in connection with their graffiti case, a fact he didn't tell me about until I flat out asked him.

"I knew that you worked with his brother," Dad explained. "I thought it best to leave you out of it."

"I just want to know what's going on," I told him. We were in the den watching the local news and waiting for Mom to get home so we could go out to dinner. Neither one of us felt like cooking, although our idea of cooking was to take something out of the freezer and shove it in the oven for twenty minutes.

"It's complicated," Dad said, putting the TV on mute. "Two of the businesses want to press charges, but one is in Tennessee and the other is in Oklahoma, so it's a jurisdiction nightmare. Ben's not looking at jail time in either case. Just some fines, probably community service."

"What about here? Is anyone in Cleary pressing charges?"

"Not yet, not that I know of. If he's charged with vandalism here, it will probably be the same result—community service and a fine."

It didn't sound to me like it was that big of a deal. Why, then, had Eli's entire family felt the need to travel all the way to Oklahoma? Eli had missed a week of school, and from what I knew of his parents, that was a big deal. There was something else to the story, I thought.

When Mom came home from work she was too tired to go out, so we ordered Chinese. Dad let me drive through the neighborhood on our way to pick up the food, but once we got to the main street he made me get out so he could take over.

"I don't know why you don't trust me," I complained.

"It's not you I don't trust," Dad said mildly. "It's everyone else on the road."

The Chinese restaurant was next door to the tuxedo shop. It was still adorned with a going-out-of-business banner, but I'd heard that sales had picked up after it had been tagged. I stared at the gorilla painted on the side wall while Dad ran in and picked up our order. I remembered the first time I'd seen the gorilla. Dad had been driving Eli home, and we'd sat in the back of the squad car and laughed at the quote painted above the gorilla's head: "They call this a monkey suit." Eli had pretended it was the first time he'd seen the mural, but he must have known that his brother had painted it.

I could see the familiar words painted near the gorilla's left foot: *Art Lies.* It didn't make sense to me. Of all the statements one could make about art, declaring that it lied seemed like the last thing an artist would say. Wasn't art supposed to reveal truth? I kept staring at those two little words as if they might reveal something more.

Dad returned with a bag full of white paper cartons, which he handed to me. I sat with the warm food in my lap, breathing in the scent of egg foo yung and fried rice. I pointed out *Art Lies* to my dad, who just nodded.

"It's his signature," he said. "All the murals have that tag."

"Even the ones in other states?"

"Yep. We checked."

Ben was weird and his signature was even weirder, I thought. Something bothered me about it, though, and it wasn't until we were pulling into our driveway that I figured it out. The letters did make sense, in a way.

Rearranged, they read: *Eli's art.*

15

AFTER SENDING THREE separate e-mails to Eli and not getting a reply, I told myself to calm down and wait. I would see Eli on Sunday and figure the whole insane, chaotic, mysterious mess out once and for all—in person. Until then, I just had to make it through Saturday without obsessing about the party, which was going to be difficult to do. The local news was covering the event because Nothing Serious, the band Tiffany's dad hired, was going to be there and they were the most famous people to ever come from—and return to—Cleary.

Both my parents were gone when I woke up on Saturday. Dad was meeting with the Werners' security team and Mom was busy at the bakery. She told her boss she was going to quit if he didn't give her the following week off. He agreed, and it helped calm her down. She was focused.

"I just need to get through Saturday," she told me the night before. "Then I can breathe easy for a while."

It seemed like everybody was just "trying to get through Saturday."

I showered and put on my most comfortable gray sweat-pants and a baggy blue T-shirt. My afternoon plans were simple: watch a ton of TV and maybe, if I felt like it, finish my history paper, which was due on Monday. I still didn't know what I wanted to write, but if I couldn't come up with anything, my plan was to turn in the original draft and hope Mr. Gildea would be feeling generous.

I was sprawled out on the couch at four in the afternoon, flipping through one infomercial after another, when the phone rang. I didn't answer. I was so comfortable and the phone was all the way across the room and I really didn't want to talk to anyone. Then I heard my mom's voice on the answering machine.

"Kate? Oh please, please be there," she said, her voice frantic. "Kate! You have to call me back as soon as you get this, okay? It's absolutely imperative that you—"

I grabbed the phone. "Mom? Are you okay?"

She began to cry. Real sobs, like she was hurt, and I panicked.

"Mom? What's wrong? You're scaring me."

"I need your help," she said finally. She was breathing funny, kind of gasping.

"Should I call Dad?" I was already searching through the list my parents kept next to the phone for my Dad's special emergency number.

"No, honey, I'm not hurt. But I need you down here right now."

"At the bakery?"

"Please. Bud was in a car accident and I can't get hold of Abby and my boss is out of town and I need your help."

"Bud was in a car accident? Is he okay?"

"It was a fender bender. He was on his way back from delivering one of the wedding cakes. He's going to be fine, but he has a concussion and I have three more cakes to deliver and they take two people to assemble and I can't do it alone." She was crying again, which was scary because Mom never cried. Ever. We could be watching the saddest movie ever made, with a dying kid or a sick puppy or both, and I would grab for a handful of tissues while she made some crack about bad acting and melodramatic endings.

"I'll be there as soon as I can," I assured her.

Since I had no car and no license, my options were to walk the two miles to Cleary Confections or ride my bike, a rusty ten-speed that was gathering dust in the garage. I didn't bother to change my clothes because I knew I was going to get sweaty riding the bike. I threw a bottle of water in my backpack and was pedaling down the driveway within five minutes. Luckily, most of the way was downhill, so it didn't take too long to get there.

The bakery was dark when I arrived, a Closed sign hanging on the front door. It wasn't even five yet, but I knew Mom had closed early because she couldn't handle any customers. I walked my bike around back. The delivery van was parked there with its back doors flung open. The doors to the bakery were open, as well. "Mom?"

She poked her head out. "Oh thank God, Kate. Help me."

I leaned my bike against the van and rushed inside, bracing myself for all the work that would need to be done. Wedding cakes were not delivered in one piece. The pieces were made separately, then assembled at the site and touched up with extra frosting. I had helped Mom once before and watched her go through the process a dozen times, so I knew that it was a delicate procedure. We began loading the separate pieces into the van. She had already loaded one cake, and the different layers sat in little white boxes, which she had color coded.

It took us twenty minutes to pack the van and get going. Mom was trying to drive while glancing at a map and fumbling with her purse and for a moment I didn't think we'd make it out of the parking lot. I tried to focus on my job, which was to sit in the back of the van and do my best to keep all the boxes from sliding around. Mom tried to drive slowly, but she was in a rush, and we seemed to hit every pothole in town.

"How much time do we have?" I yelled from the back.

"Three cakes, two hours," she replied. It usually took one hour to make sure a cake was perfectly set up. It was going to be a rough night.

Fortunately, our first delivery was easy. The cake was only four tiers and we were ten minutes early, so there was no problem. Mom began to loosen up a little after we left. "One down, two to go," she said, a note of relief in her voice.

Our second stop was more difficult, though. The bride's mother, who was wearing a ruffled red dress that made her look like a giant tomato, watched us the entire time. After the cake—which was six tiers—was carefully put together, she slowly walked around the table and inspected our work.

"It could use some more roses," she announced, fingering the pearls at her neck.

I saw Mom clench her fist and take a deep breath. I jumped in before she could say anything to Tomato Woman.

"Actually, your daughter requested a specific number of roses," I lied. "She said it was personally symbolic."

Mom gave me a shocked look. Tomato Woman looked

doubtful. "Well," she murmured, "I guess if that's what she wanted…"

I grabbed Mom by the arm and pulled her away, leaving Tomato Woman to count the buttercream roses in a fruitless attempt to figure out their symbolism.

"I hope you're not that good at lying all the time," Mom remarked as we hurried to the van.

"Only when it counts," I replied.

We had forty minutes and one delivery left, but it was the biggest cake. There were a dozen different boxes and I tried to keep both hands on the largest ones as my mom picked up speed and made a sharp right turn.

"Sorry!" she called back to me.

"Where are we going?" I was already looking forward to getting home and enjoying a bubble bath and basking in the parental brownie points I had just earned for all my hard work.

Mom said something, but I couldn't hear her.

"What?"

There were no windows in the back of the van, so I couldn't see anything, but when the road went from bumpy to smooth and my mom began to slow down, I knew we had arrived at our last location. Mom put the van in Park. I began to get up, but she stopped me.

"Kate, wait."

I was expecting her to thank me for helping her, one of her couldn't-have-done-it-without-you speeches. Instead, she apologized. "I'm sorry you had to come here like this."

"Where are we?" Through the windshield I could see tall trees twinkling with tiny gold lights and beyond them, a vast lawn. But it wasn't a lawn, I realized with a sinking feeling. It was a golf course. Specifically, the Cleary Country Club, location of Tiffany Werner's Sixteenth Birthday Spectacular. I groaned.

"Mom, no. Don't make me go in there. Please let me sit out here in the van." I worried that someone from school might see me or the camera crew would be prowling around getting footage of the party preparations.

"Just help me carry in the boxes, Kate. That's all. Ten minutes, tops. Please."

It was the way she said *please.* I knew she was exhausted and desperate and counting on me. I took a deep breath.

"Ten minutes," I said. "Let's go."

I carried one of the larger boxes through the back door leading to the kitchen. Inside, a frenzied blur of people dressed in white shirts and black pants carried trays and yelled over the sound of pots clanging and the heavy thump of bass coming from the next room. The party, I guessed, had begun early. I set down the first box on an empty table.

"No, no, no!" a woman shrieked. She was dressed like one of the servers and had her hair pulled back in a tight ponytail. "This is the cake, right?"

I nodded.

"Well, it's about time you showed up. Mrs. Werner is throwing a fit."

Mom entered holding two more boxes. "Where should we set up?" she asked.

The girl sighed and pointed to the corner. "There's the table. It's on wheels, so be careful. I'll let Mrs. Werner know you're here."

Mom had numbered the boxes. I had box number one, so

we opened it and lifted out the first section, a long rectangle iced with pale blue frosting and decorated with a hundred candy pearls. I could tell immediately that this one perfect piece had probably taken hours.

"It's gorgeous," I breathed.

"Thanks," Mom said. "Let's hope Mrs. Werner agrees with you."

A tall blonde woman entered the kitchen. She was dressed in a cream-colored silk dress that made her look like a Greek pillar. As she walked toward us, the silk rippled like liquid.

"How nice of you to finally join us," she said icily.

Mom put on her patented fake smile. "I hope we haven't inconvenienced you."

Mrs. Werner examined the first layer. "I see you managed to get the color right," she said. "Where's the rest of it?"

I hurried out back to retrieve two more boxes. When I returned, Mrs. Werner had left and Mom was assembling the second and third layers. It wasn't like a wedding cake, exactly. The layers were staggered to make it look like the cake was actually a pile of presents. Mom explained that Mr. Werner was going to place a special gift on the top tier.

"Mrs. Werner is going to be back in five minutes," Mom said. "Keep bringing in the boxes. I'll stack."

The kitchen was hot and stuffy, so I was actually happy to be able to step outside and inhale the cool night air. I collected two more boxes from the back of the van. It was dark out, but I couldn't see any stars. Distant laughter and voices echoed from the front of the building and someone, I guessed kitchen staff, was opening the Dumpster at the side of the building.

"So much for only ten minutes," I mumbled as I carried the boxes inside.

It took Mom nearly an hour to put together Tiffany's cake. It was massive. I was actually afraid that the little wheeled table wouldn't be able to hold the weight of it. Each layer was the same shade of soft blue, but the decorative patterns were different. Tiny edible pearls decorated the first tier, a design that looked like white lace was piped onto the second and a cluster of diamonds made from sugar sat on the third. Each of the twelve tiers was unique. Different size, different design. It belonged on the cover of a gourmet cooking magazine, I thought. Instead, Tiffany would take a big breath and spit all over it.

"I think this is your best work yet," I said. I was really proud of my mom.

"Thanks." She smiled. "It took forever. I almost hate to see it eaten."

"Me, too. I wish I had a camera."

Mom motioned toward her purse. "You can use the one on my phone."

I located the phone and snapped a few shots, trying to capture the cake at every angle. I wished I had a better camera, something with a higher resolution. I knew the pictures I was taking wouldn't do Mom's creation justice.

Mrs. Werner returned, this time with Monica and Mallory in tow.

"But it would be so cool!" Monica was whining.

"Please? Just this once?" Mallory pleaded.

"No one is going to hang from the balcony on a rope!" Mrs. Werner said sternly.

Before they could beg some more, Monica and Mallory saw

me. They stopped, narrowed their eyes, then turned and stomped off without another word. They were going to tell Tiffany that I was there and I hoped Mrs. Werner would approve the cake so Mom and I could leave before that happened. I didn't need an irate birthday girl storming back here with a camera crew to make a scene that would be aired later on national television. I looked down at my T-shirt, now streaked with frosting, and my baggy sweatpants. No, I definitely did not need to be on television.

"Well." Mrs. Werner was scrutinizing the cake. I held my breath and swore that if she uttered a single negative remark about Mom's hard work I would smash her perfectly coiffed head into the top tier. "I certainly had my doubts that a local baker could pull this off," Mrs. Werner said finally. "But this is good." She gave my mom a small smile. "This is very good."

I saw the relief on Mom's face. "I'm so glad you like it. Now, you'll want to start cutting here," she pointed to the corner of the bottom layer. "And careful of the dowels. There are twenty-four of them, but I'm sure the caterers have served wedding cakes before and this is similar."

Mrs. Werner frowned. "Why would the caterers cut it?"

"Well, that's what they are paid to do, isn't it?"

Mrs. Werner shook her head. "No, they *serve* the cake. You are to stay and cut it. I spoke with Sam last week. He said you would see to it that it was delivered and sliced to serve three hundred."

"Sam did not tell me that," Mom said. I knew she just wanted to get home. It was already after nine, and staying to cut the cake would be another hour's worth of work, if not more. She would need me, and I needed to become invisible as soon as humanly possible so no one from school would see me wearing dirty sweats, no makeup and a frizzy ponytail.

Mrs. Werner informed us that they would roll out the cake at ten and Mom could begin cutting immediately afterward. The kitchen staff would have the plates ready, and she could possibly spare one of the waiters to assist her. "It's a fine cake," Mrs. Werner said, "but it would be nice if you and your staff—" here she glanced at me "—would be a little more organized."

Just as she was about to leave, I heard the determined clicking of three sets of high heels. Tiffany burst into the kitchen accompanied by Monica and Mallory. A cameraman stood behind them while one scurried around to Tiffany's side.

"What is *she* doing here?" Tiffany demanded. She pointed at me but looked at her mother.

"She's part of the kitchen help, darling."

"No, she's not. She's from my school and she's trying to crash my party. Get her out. Now." Tiffany wore a strapless blue silk dress that touched the floor and a glittering tiara on her head. I hated to admit it, but she looked gorgeous.

My mom stepped in. "Kate is here to assist me."

Mrs. Werner sighed. "Well, I'm sorry, but if Tiffany wants her to leave, she'll have to go." She gave Mom one of those what-can-you-do smiles. Tiffany beamed at me, triumphant.

Mom's voice became hard. "If my daughter leaves, so do I."

Mrs. Werner's smile fizzled. "We talked about this. You stay."

"If my daughter leaves, so do I," Mom repeated. There was a warning in her voice. It was the voice of someone who'd had a rough day and wasn't willing to be pushed any further.

Mrs. Werner recognized it—all moms do—and spoke to Tiffany.

"They'll be leaving just as soon as the cake is served, darling."

Tiffany stomped her foot. "They will be leaving *now.*"

I tried to slink behind my mom, who was gripping the cake table with both hands. Mrs. Werner cleared her throat. I could tell she was trying hard not to lose control in front of the rolling cameras.

"Darling, there's something on your dress," she said.

Tiffany panicked. "What? Where?"

Mrs. Werner led Tiffany to the corner of the kitchen and whispered something to her. Tiffany motioned to her friends, and a minute later the three of them left with the camera crew trailing behind to record their every angry step. Mrs. Werner walked back to Mom and me.

"Kate will need to stay in the kitchen," she said.

"I was planning to," I told her. "I'm not really dressed for a party."

Mrs. Werner nodded and left the room. Mom let go of the table. Her face was red and she was grinding her teeth.

"Unbelievable," she muttered.

"Actually, it's completely believable." I started laughing. Mom looked at me, and then she began to laugh, too. She put one arm around my shoulder.

"Thank you for not being a spoiled brat."

"Did I have that option?" I joked.

Mom looked at me. "I mean it, Kate. You're always there when we need you. You work hard. You make your dad and me proud."

I smiled. "Thanks. I guess I needed to hear that."

The catering staff was busy bringing in dirty plates and loading the massive dishwashers at one end of the room. I looked around for something to snack on, but the silver hors d'oeuvres trays had been picked clean.

A few minutes before ten, Mr. Werner strode into the kitchen. He was holding a small velvet box. "Now where should this go, exactly?" he mused as he peered at the top of the cake. He flipped open the lid to reveal a set of car keys attached to a diamond chain. He winked at my mom. "Some night, huh?"

Mom automatically flashed one of her fake smiles. "It sure is."

I could hear the sarcasm in her voice. Mom helped Mr. Werner position Tiffany's present on the top tier. They placed sparklers around it, then Mr. Werner glanced at his watch.

"It's time," he announced. He clapped his hands together. "Attention!" The kitchen staff stopped moving. "I expect all of you to sing. Let's go."

I walked alongside the cart as Mom pushed the cake toward the main room. It wobbled slightly, so we moved slowly. As Mr. Werner opened the doors, I stayed behind and watched. Mr. Werner led the way, followed by my mom and a dozen waiters. It was like a little parade. The lights in the main room dimmed, the crowd hushed and the band began to play the birthday song. I was supposed to close the doors behind everyone, but I couldn't resist. I had to get a peek at the party. I waited a moment, then poked my head out.

What I saw took my breath away.

I HAD ATTENDED FIVE WEDDINGS, three graduation parties and one prom in my life. They were all formal and beautiful and expensive celebrations, each one memorable in its own way. Not one of them came close to being as stunning as Tiffany Werner's birthday party.

The main reception room of the Cleary Country Club had been transformed into something that looked like it belonged in a fairy tale. A high-priced fairy tale.

Layers of pale blue netting had been draped across the room and over the walls, giving everything a soft, elegant feel. The tables featured silver bowls filled with dozens of white roses and clusters of flickering votive candles. The chandeliers above each table had been decorated with strands of faux pearls, and the chairs had been covered with blue silk tied back with pearl-laced bows.

Six huge video screens had been set up throughout the space. Pictures of Tiffany as a happy little girl morphed into glamorous shots of her at sixteen, posing in a slinky blue dress and gazing into the camera with a sexy, solemn stare.

I remembered Tiffany's dress code: no blue and no white. There were a lot of red and black and green dresses. I spotted

Trent in his pink tuxedo. He was dancing in the middle of the room, attracting attention as usual. His friends wore the same kind of thrift-store tuxedo, but in different colors like butter-yellow and olive-green and even bright orange. I didn't see Eli, Brady or Reva, to my relief.

Everyone wore the blue bracelets included as part of the invitation. The effect of everyone wearing the same piece of plastic was a weird one. It reminded me of nature shows I'd seen where the animals were tagged so scientists could track them.

Waiters removed china plates from the tables as half the student body converged around a large stage at the front of the room. Mr. Werner grabbed a microphone and asked his "little girl" to come up onstage. Everyone cheered as Tiffany walked onto the stage and over to her father. The cake was rolled out in front of her, the sparklers on top illuminating the smile stretched across her face.

After the sparklers fizzled out, Tiffany plucked the shiny silver keys from the top tier. She licked off a dab of frosting that clung to them and waved the keys in the air while the crowd applauded. I slipped back into the kitchen, worried that I might be caught on film, an outsider trying to look in.

Mom wheeled the cake back into the kitchen and we immediately began the process of cutting and serving. The waiters arranged little silver plates on their trays, and my mom would cut a thick square from one layer and place it directly onto the plate. When the plates were full, the tray went out. I sliced into another layer, and one of the waiters worked on yet another. I kept checking how my mom was cutting so I didn't slice pieces that were too big or too small.

"This needs to feed three hundred," she reminded me grimly.

We were moving fast, but it wasn't fast enough. The waiters were grabbing the trays the second they were full and scurrying out to the main room. I didn't let the commotion bother me. I'd worked at Something's Brewing on days that were nonstop crazy, and I had to balance hot drinks and avoid crashing into Eli. This felt similar, except that I had to keep my arm from brushing against the frosting and avoid accidentally spearing one of the bustling waiters with the cake knife I was holding.

Mrs. Werner looked in on us a few times. "We'll have enough, won't we?" she kept asking. Mom didn't bother to answer.

Finally, we were done. The cake had been served. Three hundred and four pieces, each one about the same size, each one served on a silver plate and placed in front of a person who had no idea how much work it had taken to get it there. The three smallest tiers remained, and my mom cut them into pieces in case there was a demand for seconds. I began to clean up our supplies.

"I'll take these out to the van," I told my mom after I collected all the pastry bags and dowels and tubes of extra icing. "Back in a minute."

She grunted something but was too preoccupied with finishing her job to notice me. I couldn't wait to leave. I wanted to forget the entire intense evening. I decided I would call Lan and cancel our overnight plans so I could just crash at home. I knew she wouldn't mind because she was out with Brady.

Outside, it had grown chilly and quiet. I loaded our stuff into the back of the van and sat down on the hard metal bumper, glad to have a minute to myself. From the dull roar near the front of the building, I guessed that Tiffany was being led outside to see her new car. It was probably a convertible with an enormous bow wrapped around the hood. I wondered if she would scream when she saw her gift or play it cool, as though she had expected it all along. "Guess I'll find out when it's on TV," I said to myself. I hoped that she wouldn't spread a rumor on Monday that I had tried to crash her party, but if she did, I was prepared to deny everything.

I was about to go back into the kitchen to help Mom when someone came running from the side of the building.

"Reva? Is that you?" I didn't think Reva was going to attend the party, but there she was, wearing a clingy black dress and long satin gloves.

She rushed toward me. "Oh, Kate, thank God!" She looked frantic.

"What's wrong?"

"It's Eli. He's hurt. You have to help him!"

My heart skipped a beat. "What happened? Where is he?"

"Over there, by the Dumpster. I'll call an ambulance. Just go!"

I ran in the direction Reva had pointed to while she hurried inside to call for help. The Dumpster was against the side wall, away from all the lights.

"Eli?"

At first, I couldn't see anything in the dark except for the black outline of the Dumpster against the brick wall. I looked around. Was I in the wrong place? My foot bumped against something that rolled away and hit the wall with a hollow, metallic sound. There was a white shape in the corner, and I thought it was Eli huddled against the Dumpster. It looked like he was wearing a white T-shirt.

"Oh, no," I whispered. Something was definitely wrong. I went over to him, knelt down and put my shaking hand on his back. Only it wasn't him. It was a wadded-up bedsheet. I lifted the sheet and realized something was wrapped inside it. When I stood up, three metal canisters tumbled out.

I picked up one of the canisters. I didn't know what was going on, but Eli wasn't here. Had he dragged himself to the front of the building? I scanned the ground for blood, anything to give me a clue as to where Eli was. I had taken only a few steps when I saw the lights.

It didn't make sense to me, at first. One second it was pitch-black and the next, red-and-blue lights were blinding me. I put one hand up to my face.

"Hold it right there!"

A man was yelling at me. I put my hand down. I was still holding the sheet and one canister, and I realized the light was coming from a car parked directly in front of me.

"Kate?"

The voice was familiar, but I still couldn't see past the lights to the speaker. A man approached me.

"George?" It was one of the officers my dad worked with.

"Kate, what have you done?" He sounded worried.

"My friend Eli. He's hurt," I stammered.

My eyes finally adjusted to the glare of the headlights and I could see George more clearly. "Just stay there, Kate," he said.

I could hear voices. People were walking toward us. My first thought was that more help had arrived. Then I saw that the group headed in our direction was dressed up. I almost groaned out loud. Three hundred students from Cleary High School were going to see me at my worst, and they would all think I was trying to crash Tiffany's precious party.

I felt like a trapped animal and debated running back to my mom's van. It seemed like only seconds before a huge crowd had gathered behind the police car. They were pointing at me. Some looked angry while others were snickering.

"Can you believe it was her all along?"

"Tiffany's gonna freak."

"She is *so* busted."

They weren't really looking at me, I realized. They were looking at something behind me. I turned. There, on the wall, was a gorilla.

And I was holding an empty can of spray paint.

IT ACTUALLY DIDN'T DAWN ON ME that I had been set up until I spotted Reva standing near the side of the crowd. She was smirking. I put the pieces together in one sudden, shattering second: Reva had framed me. She had, in the end, gotten her revenge on me for supposedly stealing her boyfriend, who was not injured and bleeding somewhere, but probably at home, oblivious to the drama unfolding at the Cleary Country Club. It would have been more humane, I thought, if Reva had simply slashed my throat with her nails.

I looked at the crowd. They looked back at me, waiting.

"I didn't do this," I said, but my voice was barely audible.

I was horribly aware of the hundreds of eyes focused on me. They were judging me, and I felt totally exposed. I took a step back until I could feel the wall behind me and I leaned against it, afraid that my wobbly legs might give way at any second.

The crowd began to part for someone. I could hear Tiffany's voice before I saw her, and I closed my eyes and wished that I could disappear or melt into a puddle or sprout wings and fly away.

"You."

Tiffany stood about eight feet from me. The TV crew was positioned behind her, and the intense lights from their cameras hurt my eyes.

"I knew you were jealous, but I had no idea how much. You did that to my car, didn't you?"

I had no idea what she was talking about. All I knew was that Tiffany was angry, and I had seen her angry before. Her voice was a deadly growl and, if looks could kill, I would have turned to a pile of ashes in that moment. She was headed for meltdown mode, despite the cameras and the crowd. Or maybe they just added to her outrage and she wanted to make a scene worthy of her audience. Either way, she stepped toward me, clenching her fists and trembling with raw rage.

George stepped in. I think he saw the potential for not only a homicide but some kind of crazed teenage uprising. "This way, Kate," he said, ushering me to his squad car. Something crunched under my foot. I looked down and saw that a piece of the gorilla stencil was stuck to my shoe. I bent down and peeled it off, then handed it to George. Half the crowd began to boo while the other half cheered.

Mom heard the commotion and walked over to George and me. "What on earth is going on here?"

"I'm going to have Kate take a seat," George said, opening the back door to his car. "It's for her safety."

"For her what?"

While I sat in the backseat listening to the crackling police scanner, George talked with Mom. More police arrived, my dad among them. I tried not to look out the window, but it was hard—people were pressing up against the squad car and taking pictures of me with their cell phones. I put a hand to my forehead and tried to shield my face, but it was useless. Everyone had seen me dressed in dirty sweats, holding a spray-paint can. I had never before been the focus of so much unwanted attention. It was beyond my worst fears and felt a thousand times worse than I could have ever imagined.

"So this is public humiliation," I said to myself.

I had spent so much of my life avoiding the spotlight, only to have it shoved—literally—in my face.

Mr. and Mrs. Werner appeared off to the side. I watched from the backseat as Mrs. Werner held a sobbing Tiffany. Mr. Werner went over to my dad. I couldn't hear what he was saying, but he didn't look happy. There was a lot of pointing in my direction and raised voices. After a while, George got back in the car.

"Let's get you out of here, Kate."

I nodded. We weren't able to pull away immediately because of the mob surrounding the car. George inched the cruiser forward, its blue lights flashing. I caught a glimpse of Trent in his pink tuxedo. He was talking on a cell phone, one finger pressed against his ear to block out the noise of the crowd. Reva stood behind him, smiling as she examined one of her long fingernails. I felt a surge of fury toward her. She had done this to me. She had created this mess and now she was just going to stand there enjoying my mortification and there was nothing I could do about it.

I closed my eyes and leaned my head back against the seat. It was a long ride to the station.

The evidence was in my favor—sort of. There were at least a dozen witnesses who saw me in the kitchen all night, so I had a solid alibi. I had to sit in a tiny room at the station and tell my story about a hundred times and answer the same questions over and over, but I didn't mind because I just wanted to get everything cleared up. It helped that my parents believed me.

Of course, there were spray-paint cans with my fingerprints on them. And, I discovered as I sat under the fluorescent lights of the station, a smear of black paint across my sweat pants. In a few months I would be on national television looking like I spent a week living under a bridge. If I had been guilty, that alone would have been punishment enough.

As I answered the barrage of questions the police threw at me, I had a few of my own. I wondered how Reva had gotten her hands on the stencil and how long she had planned her revenge. I wondered about Eli and where he was. And, as the police kept asking me about it, I wondered what had happened to Tiffany's birthday car. Had Reva damaged the expensive gift first in an attempt to frame me for even more serious charges? I tried telling the police about Reva, but they didn't seem to believe me. She was an invited guest at the party and I was not. George promised to look into it, and I knew he would. Still, that didn't mean much. If Reva was smart—and I was sure she was—she would have gotten rid of anything that could remotely connect her to what happened.

It was well after midnight before they let me go. There would be an investigation, as both the country club and the Werners wanted to press charges. I was too tired at that point to care very much. I fell asleep on the ride home in my dad's car and slept until noon the next day.

THE RINGING PHONE WOKE ME. I rolled over and grabbed it, still groggy.

"Hello?" I mumbled.

"Kate! I was so worried! Are you okay? Did they make you sit in jail all night?"

"Hi, Lan."

"What happened?"

I rubbed at my eyes. Sunlight blared at me from the window. "It was a mess." I didn't feel like rehashing my story for the millionth time. I knew I would need to tell it at school on Monday to anyone who would listen. In fact, I thought miserably, I'd probably be repeating it for the rest of my high school career. Some people would love me for what I didn't do, and some would hate me. Maybe I could get Eden to do a feature on my side of the story, I thought. It was definitely newsworthy.

"But you're okay?"

"Physically, yes." I sighed. "I'm never going to live this down."

"Well, I know you're innocent. When I saw you sitting in the back of that police car, I freaked, okay? Really freaked. They should never have dragged you off like that."

I sat up in bed, fully awake now. "You saw me? How?"

"Oh. Right. Well, Brady and I were kind of there."

"Kind of?"

"We were there. We messed with Tiffany's new car."

I remembered the officers asking me questions about the car, but I didn't understand what they were talking about and they didn't offer any details.

"What did you do, Lan?"

"Technically, it was Brady. I just created a distraction so security wouldn't notice."

"So security wouldn't notice what, exactly?"

"We didn't wreck anything, promise. Brady just wiped Vaseline all over the windows."

I couldn't help it—I laughed. Lan explained how she pretended to be throwing up in the bushes. When one of the security guards came over to check on her, Brady smeared the clear jelly across the front and side windows of the cherry-red convertible. It wouldn't do any permanent damage, but it would take forever to get the stuff completely off, and Tiffany wouldn't be able to drive her fancy new gift until it had been thoroughly cleaned.

"The police asked me about the car," I told Lan after she finished.

"I'm sorry. Look, Brady and I will admit to it, okay? You won't get in trouble."

"I'm already in trouble."

"This will all get cleared up, though. Really."

I wanted to talk to Lan some more, but I also wanted to find out as much information as I could from my parents.

"I'll let you know when I hear something," I promised.

"It'll be okay, Kate. I know it."

I hung up the phone. "I'm glad one of us does," I mumbled.

After taking a scalding-hot shower and throwing on a pair of jeans and a sweatshirt, I went downstairs. I could smell coffee, and a box of doughnuts sat on the kitchen counter. I grabbed a coconut one, poured myself a glass of juice and went to the family room, where Mom was sitting on the sofa with a steaming mug.

"You're up," she said.

"I shouldn't have slept so long." I sat next to her and took a bite out of my doughnut. "You could have woke me."

"I just got up myself," she said, sipping her coffee.

"Where's Dad?"

"He went in early this morning. He's going to try and sort this whole mess out."

I sighed. "That's going to take a long time, isn't it?"

Mom patted my leg. "We'll get through it, hon. Promise."

I hated the fact that she was giving me one of her fake smiles, like she wanted to reassure me that everything was going to work out fine when, in fact, I was screwed. I decided to play along, though, and gave her a fake smile of my own.

"You're right," I lied. "It'll be okay."

18

I REALLY DIDN'T THINK my parents would force me to go to school on Monday. They knew I had been framed and believed I was innocent. I thought I would get some sympathy points for being victimized and publicly humiliated, but no such luck.

"You're going," Dad informed me Sunday night.

"Everyone at school thinks I'm a party-crashing vandal with poor fashion sense!" I cried. "Haven't I been traumatized enough?"

"Only guilty people avoid public situations. You're not guilty. You're going."

I appealed to Mom, but she and Dad had this annoying deal: when one of them laid down the law, the other had to support the decision, no matter how wrong, unfair or downright cruel it might be.

"You're going, but I'll give you a ride," Mom said. She was taking her much-needed vacation all week. Her boss had called a few times because he was short staffed (since Bud was still recovering from his fender bender), but Mom wouldn't answer the phone. I tensed every time I heard it ring, not because of Mom's boss, but because I was hoping it would be Eli. He knew what had happened—I was sure of it—and I was waiting for him to check on me. By the time I went to bed on Sunday night, I still hadn't heard from him.

I got up early on Monday and spent extra time making sure I looked presentable. I wanted to wipe away the grungy image of myself that most of the party guests had witnessed, so I wore a crisp white blouse and my favorite khakis.

Mom took her time driving me to school and let me linger in the car for a few minutes so I could avoid the morning hallway crowds and walk right into class. I didn't want to give anyone a chance to ask me about Saturday night. I didn't know what people had heard: was I just a rebellious prankster, like Trent, or a Tiffany wannabe desperately trying to gain attention for herself? I knew a jury of my peers had already sentenced me. I just didn't know the verdict.

I was aware that everyone had been talking about me because it became eerily quiet as soon as I walked into first period history. I slid into my desk just as the bell rang. Mr. Gildea took attendance while people whispered behind me.

"She spent the night in jail."

"The Werners are suing her for destruction of property."

"Not even Daddy can bail her out of this one."

The last comment stung, but I pretended that I was too pre-occupied with my fascinating notebook to hear it. Lan nudged me and smiled. I couldn't force a smile in return, so instead I just nodded.

Tiffany strode in a minute later. She handed Mr. Gildea a late pass and walked to her desk. She didn't look at me. She didn't look at anyone.

"Well, then, let's begin," said Mr. Gildea. He was wearing

his orange-and-green tie. I prayed that he wouldn't start class with another debate. I had witnessed Tiffany's volcanic temper twice now, and I didn't want her to erupt again.

"I trust you have completed your essay revisions? Pass them forward, please."

I felt my stomach tighten. Not only had I forgotten the revisions, I had left my original essay at home. I had nothing to turn in, and Mr. Gildea had a strict late policy. Even if I handed it in by lunchtime, I would lose points.

The rest of class went by in a boring blur. When the bell rang, I told Lan I'd see her later and waited in my seat. I wanted Tiffany to leave the room first so I could avoid her. Also, I needed to talk to Mr. Gildea about my paper.

After the room cleared out, I approached Mr. Gildea's desk.

"Yes, Miss Morgan?" He was writing in his lesson plan book and didn't look up.

"I have a question about my paper."

Mr. Gildea set his pen down and looked at me. "You are referring to the one you didn't turn in this morning?"

"Um, yeah. That one."

Mr. Gildea sat back in his chair. "I understand you had a rather hectic weekend," he said. "I suppose I can give you an extension, provided, of course, that you turn in a complete revision. I'll deduct ten points, however. Sound fair?"

"Yes. Very fair. Thank you, Mr. Gildea."

I was relieved that I had bought myself a little more time, but I knew I had to turn in something really good, and I was coming up blank on brilliant ideas.

Throughout the day I tried to avoid spending too much time in the hallways. I was always the last to leave class, which meant

I had to rush to my next class to make it on time. Still, I heard the loud whispers. Some people smiled at me while others glared.

I looked forward to lunch only because it meant that I would be surrounded by friends. I tried to sneak into the cafeteria through a rarely used side door, hoping I wouldn't attract a lot of attention, but I bumped into a chair, causing it to slide across the floor with a loud screech. I hurried to my table and sat down.

Eden was waiting for me, her pen poised. "You're my lead story for this week," she said. "Start talking."

I glanced to my right. "Do you know if Reva or Eli is here?" Once again, I was aware of the people looking in my direction.

"Reva wasn't in homeroom. Don't know about Eli."

"Brady said Eli would be here today, but he was coming in late," Lan said.

I was glad that Reva wasn't in school. My dad had mentioned that she was going to be questioned again. Maybe she was sitting in a holding cell, I thought hopefully.

I gave Eden my story while I picked at my lunch. I had no appetite.

"Just so you know, I can't mention Reva by name," she said as I concluded my version of events.

"What? Why not?" Unless people knew who had really been behind Tiffany's Birthday Debacle, they would think it was me.

"It's a liability thing. I'll have to refer to her as 'an unnamed junior.' Trust me, though. It'll get people talking. They'll know it was her within an hour."

I thought about it and realized that people were much more likely to believe a rumor than something they read in the school paper.

"Have you spoken to Tiffany yet?" I asked.

"No. I tried calling her yesterday, but no luck. I'll track her down later today."

Even when the truth was completely revealed, I knew Tiffany would still hate me. It didn't really matter, but I'd rather be hated for something I did do than for something I didn't.

The bell rang and I stood up. Before I could throw away my uneaten sandwich and carrot sticks, though, Principal Carter walked over to my table.

"Miss Morgan, I need you to come with me, please." He held out one arm and motioned toward the side doors, away from the crowd. I stole one quick, panicked glance at Lan before going with Carter.

He said nothing as we walked through the hallways. I was worried—what was going on? Usually when someone was called down to the office they sent one of the vice principals or an office assistant to get them. Carter only came for the really serious stuff, like if someone was being busted for drugs.

When we arrived at the main office he asked me to take a seat near his secretary's desk. He went into his office and I sat next to a kid holding an ice pack to his nose and waited. A few minutes later, Principal Carter emerged from his office holding a stack of manila file folders. I started to stand, but he didn't look at me; instead, he walked down the administrative hallway and into one of the conference rooms. I could hear voices coming from the room. Someone was shouting.

"Some meeting," the kid next to me said as he rearranged his ice pack. "They've been yelling like that for half an hour."

I didn't know what was going on, but I knew it had to do with the party. I was about to ask the secretary how long she thought I would be waiting when the conference-room door flew open.

"I cannot *believe* you are doing this to me!" a girl shrieked.

I knew that voice.

It was Reva's voice.

A second later she came storming out of the room. Her mascara ran down her face in jagged streaks and she wiped at her nose with the back of her hand. When she saw me, she stopped.

"You won, okay? You won. *Happy?*"

I was shocked by the venom in her voice. The guy next to me sat up straight and looked around like he was trying to find the nearest exit.

"What did I win?" I asked. It just slipped out, and it was obviously the wrong thing to say, because Reva glared at me and opened her mouth like she was going to start screaming. Before she could, though, an older woman came out of the room.

"Reva? Honey? Let's go." I guessed that the woman, who was short and wore her silver hair in a tiny bun, was her grandmother. I watched Reva as she furiously shoved the school's front doors with both hands, causing them to rattle.

Bloody Nose Guy was watching, too. "Whoa," he said. "Whatever you won, you might want to give it back."

Principal Carter called me in to the conference room and I got up, a little shaky and very uncertain about what was happening. There was quite a crowd seated around the long oval table in the center of the room. One of the vice principals sat next to George, who was wearing his police uniform. I recognized Mr. Werner from the party. He was dressed in a dark suit and sat next to the principal. Another man, also dressed in a suit and tie, sat to his left. I wondered if he was the Werners' lawyer. At the end of the table sat my parents. Dad wasn't in uniform; instead, he was wearing jeans and a wrinkled plaid shirt. I took a seat next to him and he squeezed my shoulder.

"Now, then," Principal Carter began. He opened one of the manila folders in front of him. "Kate. We have some things we need to clear up and we're hoping you can answer some questions for us."

"Okay," I said, glancing at Mom. She smiled, but it was strained.

"You were at Tiffany Werner's birthday party to help your mother, is that correct?"

"Yes." I felt like I was on trial. Mr. Werner's lawyer was jotting notes on a yellow pad of paper.

"When, exactly, did you first see Reva Abbott?"

I recited my story once again. Principal Carter wrote things down in his folder. When I finished speaking, the lawyer addressed me.

"Is it true, Miss Morgan, that you were not invited to the party?"

"Just a minute," Dad said. He sounded mad. "We already established that it was not my daughter who painted that wall. How is this question at all relevant?"

Now it really did feel like I was on trial and Dad was serving as my attorney.

"We still have not determined who vandalized Miss Werner's car," the lawyer said smoothly. He turned to me and waited.

"Actually, I *was* invited to the party," I said, looking the lawyer in the eyes. "I chose not to go after Tiffany made a racist comment about my best friend, who is Vietnamese."

"My daughter would never do such a thing!" Mr. Werner exploded.

Principal Carter opened another folder. "Actually, Tiffany's history teacher filled out a report. We tried to contact you about it last week, but you didn't return our calls."

"I never touched Tiffany's car," I said. "I never even saw it."

There was no way I was going to mention Brady and Lan. The lawyer asked me more questions about what I saw and when I saw it, but I didn't actually witness anything, so I couldn't add much to what I had already told them. After a few minutes, Principal Carter closed his folder.

"I think we're done, then," he said. "Thank you for coming in, Kate."

"Now wait just a minute!" Mr. Werner yelled. "Someone is responsible! Someone is going to pay for the detailing on my daughter's car!"

"Yes, someone is responsible," George said. "It's just not Kate."

"Someone also owes Kate an apology," Mom pointed out. She stared hard at the Werners. Mr. Werner looked away while Mrs. Werner fidgeted with her diamond tennis bracelet.

Their lawyer shuffled some papers. "Of course we regret that this situation occurred," he said. "It has been difficult for everyone involved."

"That's not an apology," Dad said.

Mom put her hand on his arm. "Don't bother. We can't ask the Werners to show us a shred of decency. They are clearly unfamiliar with the concept."

The Werners looked furious but said nothing. My parents stood and so did I. Principal Carter walked out with us. He shook my parents' hands in the hallway.

"Thank you again for coming in." He turned to his secretary. "I need to know where I can find Tiffany Werner," he said. She nodded and began typing on her computer. "And please give Miss Morgan a late pass to class," he added.

After I got my pass I walked with my parents to the lobby. "I don't really understand what just happened in there," I said.

Dad smiled. "What happened is that you have been cleared of all charges."

He explained that the police looked at the footage taken by the camera crew. I was on there, of course, in all my bedraggled glory. The tapes were time stamped and showed that I was in the kitchen throughout the evening. I was even visible peeking out at the crowd as everyone sang the birthday song, which would have made it impossible for me to paint the wall.

"More important is what the tapes didn't show," Dad said. He told me that the only time Reva was caught on camera was after the graffiti had been discovered. They couldn't find any trace of her inside the country club. She had denied everything, of course, but panicked when her grandmother, convinced of her granddaughter's innocence, agreed to let the police search Reva's car.

"George found evidence in the car. She had paint and pieces of the stencil."

"Stencil?" I asked.

"It's pretty amazing, really. There are four segments. She pieced them together like a puzzle, taped it to the wall and spray-painted it."

Reva still wasn't willing to take the blame, though. She claimed that the stencil belonged to Eli and that he had put it in her car without her knowledge.

"George will be speaking to Eli later," Dad said. "We think he and his brother are involved with all this, but to what extent, we're not sure."

"There's something I don't understand," I said. "How did Reva even know I was going to be at the party? I wasn't supposed to be there."

"She wouldn't say, but your friend Brady noticed her earlier that night. He thinks Reva was actually following Lan, and that her original plan was to set her up. I guess Reva was trying to cause some problems for Lan and Brady."

"She probably thought that if Lan and Brady broke up, I wouldn't want to hang around with Eli as much," I mused. "So it was just her wonderful luck that I was there?"

"Seems like it."

We heard people approaching and turned to see Principal Carter leading Tiffany to the conference room.

"Looks like Tiffany is going to have a meeting about that report your history teacher submitted," Mom said. She shook her head. "I never want to work for people like that again. They threatened not to pay for the cake, can you believe it? Of course, we already had their credit card number."

I said goodbye to my parents and reminded them I had to work after school. They said we would all go out to a nice dinner after I got home. Mom hugged me. "We're just so relieved this is over," she said.

It didn't feel over to me, though. I needed to talk to Eli. He was the only one who could answer all the questions that remained, including one that was particularly important to me: where did we go from here?

19

Bonnie was waiting for me when I got to Something's Brewing.

"Kate, dear, I need to rush out for a little bit," she said as she handed me a caramel latte.

"Is everything okay?"

She grabbed her jacket off a chair. "Everything's fine. My daughter's car broke down across town. I'll pick her up and be back within an hour. Think you can manage on your own?"

I had never worked at Something's Brewing by myself. As long as there wasn't a sudden surge of caffeine addicts, I knew I would be fine.

A few cars pulled up right after Bonnie left, but it wasn't too crazy. I had just sat down to finish my caramel latte when I saw Brady's car pull into the parking lot. Eli got out of the passenger seat and said something to Brady, who then left. I went to the back door and opened it.

"Hey," he said as I held open the door.

"Hey."

We walked down the little hallway and I sat down on a chair while he stood against the wall. I explained that Bonnie was running an errand. He nodded. It was awkward. I had been waiting so long to talk to him one-on-one and now that he was right in front of me, I didn't know what to say. I waited for him to go first.

"It's been a crazy day," he said. "Crazy couple of weeks, actually."

"Yep." I stared into my nearly empty cup.

"Kate, I'm really sorry. Everything's a mess and it's all my fault. I'm sure you have a ton of questions."

I looked at him. "Yes, I do."

He ran a hand through his hair. "Okay, where do I begin? I want to tell you everything. Right here, right now."

"Start at the beginning."

Eli pulled the only other chair in the room over to him so he was sitting directly across from me. "I've been researching colleges for a while now," he began. "I want to get into a really good school for computer graphics. They all require portfolios, and I needed something to help mine stand out."

"And you came up with gorillas?"

"Yeah. My brother helped me. I designed the stencil and he produced it when he was working at that sign shop. We set up a team, too, to help with carrying out each of our location targets."

"How did you pick the locations?" I asked.

"We looked for abandoned buildings, mainly. That way, we weren't hurting anybody. We did the school because that wall was already ruined, and we figured no one would really care."

Eli said that each member of his "team" had a different job: one would hold the stencil while the other one taped it to the wall. Eli would spray the paint. They did it that way so each gorilla only took a minute to complete and they could get away quickly. They documented each mural for Eli's college portfolio.

"Let me guess. Trent and Brady were on your team?"

"At first it was just the three of us, but then Reva found out about it." He sighed. "That's when things with her got bad. She knew I wanted to break up, but she said if I did, she'd bust all of us, my brother included."

I set my empty cup down. "Well, nothing like a little blackmail to help keep a relationship together."

He stood up and paced. "The thing is, I started doing it just for my portfolio. But then I saw the reaction it got and it became something more to me."

"What did it become?"

"A kind of protest, I think. I mean, you go through each and every day knowing what you'll do, what you'll see. I liked shaking up the routine. I liked that people actually stopped and looked at the places around them hoping something new would be there."

He stopped pacing and looked at me. "I liked that you noticed it, too, and that you thought about it."

I smiled. "I did think about it. When I wasn't thinking about you, that is."

Eli smiled back at me. Then he shook his head. "Now it's a mess, though. My brother was arrested and we don't know what kind of sentence they'll give him. Reva was suspended for the gorillas on the school—they thought she did it—but I cleared that up this afternoon so now I'm really in trouble."

"Define trouble."

"My parents grounded me until the end of the year. Carter

gave me an in-school suspension, and I also have to complete a hundred hours of custodial service at school this summer. I haven't heard yet about the legal charges."

"Let's hope this gets you into a really, really good school."

He laughed. "That would be nice."

"Did they ask you about Tiffany's car?"

"Yeah. I confessed."

"What?" I exclaimed. "Lan said she and Brady did it."

"They did, but I figured since I was already in so much trouble, I might as well take the blame for it."

"That was decent of you," I said. Eli was a good guy, I thought. But one thing still bothered me. "Why were you in Oklahoma for so long?" I asked. "And why did you wait so long to contact me? Couldn't you have told me most of this last week?"

"Oklahoma was crazy," Eli said, shaking his head. "We had to wait to see how my brother would be charged. My parents had him out on bail, which was good, but then we had to wait for a court date, and they decided we were going to stay together as a family. They didn't want to let either one of us out of their sight for a minute."

"Were they worried you and Ben would go on a painting spree?"

Eli smiled. "I guess." His expression turned serious once again. "As for not contacting you...Kate, I really wanted to. But I was worried about putting you in the middle. I didn't know if your dad was involved with the investigation, and I wanted to keep you out of it just in case he was."

A car pulled up to the window and I stood. When the driver ordered four banana lattes, Eli went to work steaming milk while I took the customer's money. For a moment, it was just like old times.

After the customer left, I thanked Eli for helping me. "You know, I've never actually tried a banana latte," I confessed.

"Then I'll make one for you," Eli said with a flourish of his arm, "and it will be the greatest drink you have ever tasted."

I giggled and sat down to watch him work. He was wearing a purple T-shirt and I loved the way it clung to his back. It would be so nice, I thought, if we could just erase the past few weeks and go back to that moment in the car when we first kissed. But we couldn't, and no matter how much I wanted things to be perfect between the two of us, the simple fact was that they weren't.

Eli handed me the warm cup and pulled his chair closer to mine.

"I've reached my latte limit for the day," I joked. I didn't take a sip right away. I wanted it to cool off a little first.

"So, are we okay now?" He was staring at me, and I self-consciously tucked a strand of hair behind my ear.

"I would like everything to be okay," I said, looking into his brown eyes. "But the truth is, I'm having a hard time with all this. You were secretive and distant and I was totally confused and hurt for a while. Those feelings aren't just going to vanish instantly."

"I understand." Eli nodded sadly.

"But there are also the feelings I had for you before all of this happened, and those aren't going to vanish, either."

He grinned. "I'm glad to hear that. So where does that leave us now?"

"I don't know," I admitted. I reached for his hand. "You

know what I want? I want a relationship that starts off right, that doesn't include a lot of baggage or angry exes or damaged feelings."

"Is that possible?"

"I don't know. Maybe, though, over time. Think we can start over?"

He brought my hand to his lips and kissed it. "I'd love to."

ELI STAYED WITH ME throughout the rest of my shift. Bonnie was thrilled to see him. Eli told her that he would need to come back to work soon. "I have a lot of fines I need to pay," he explained.

"There's always a place for you here, dear," Bonnie said, hugging him. "And I never paid you for the new sign, did I? So maybe that will help."

"New sign?" I asked.

Bonnie gave Eli a worried look. "Does she know?"

Eli nodded. "Tell her."

"I knew Eli was painting the gorillas so I asked him to paint me one. I thought it would help business." She smiled and patted Eli's shoulder. "And it has, dear. I can't thank you enough."

"How did you know it was him?" I asked.

"Call it a hunch." She winked. "That and he left his computer open one day."

I was happy that I would be working with Eli again, especially since he was grounded and work would be the only time we would be spending together until the end of the school year.

Both my parents came to pick me up after my shift so we

could drive to dinner. They saw me kiss Eli on the cheek, and as soon as I got in the car, they bombarded me with a million questions. I calmly told them that Eli and I were just friends, but there was a chance we would start dating in a few months.

"Too bad he's a vandal." Dad sighed. "I might have really liked him."

Mom gave him a playful punch to the shoulder. "I think he's sweet. He took responsibility for his actions. And he wasn't doing it to be malicious."

"That doesn't mean he needs to date my daughter," Dad grumbled, but I knew he wasn't really angry. He was only doing the concerned dad thing.

"We're just friends right now," I reminded them. "Nothing else."

We ate dinner at Mom's favorite Italian restaurant and talked about other things. I was full from lasagna and salad and bread but was considering a thick slab of tiramisu when Dad asked about school and I remembered the history paper. I couldn't put it off any longer.

As soon as we got home, I went to my computer. I spent hours on it, writing and rewriting several drafts, but nothing sounded satisfactory to me. I couldn't express what I really wanted to say and I was beyond frustrated. It wasn't just that I wanted a good grade. I felt like I had something to say about art, that it was personal and mattered to me. I wanted to define art more for myself than for Mr. Gildea's class.

After three hours I was ready to give up. No matter what I wrote, it wouldn't be good enough. Then I spotted my digital camera. I opened up the picture files on my computer and searched through all the images I'd taken in the past few months, starting with first shots on Christmas morning, right after my parents gave the camera to me. I took the rest after school began in January. There was a photo of the gorillas on the wall. One picture showed Lan wearing a pink orchid pin she had made. In another, Eden bent over a stack of newspapers. I smiled. I wasn't going to write a definition of art, after all. I was going to show it.

Three Months Later

LAN ARRIVED AT MY HOUSE an hour early. "I made banana spring rolls," she announced, holding a foil-covered casserole dish. Mom had set up a table for snacks, and I placed Lan's dessert next to the bowls of chips and plates of sliced vegetables and cheese cubes. Mom had gone to a lot of work for just a few guests, but I knew why. Ever since she'd quit her job at Cleary Confections and started her own cake business, she'd been gone a lot, and making a fuss over my simple get-together was her way of trying to make it up to me.

"The guys won't be here for another hour," I told Lan.

"I know, but I wanted to see you. Don't you have new pictures to show me?"

I went to my room and came back with a fat envelope stuffed with photographs I had printed out earlier in the day. I handed the envelope to Lan, who began to sift through them.

"This is a nice one," she said, holding up a picture I took

at prom. In it, Brady was beaming at Lan as they danced. She was looking right at the camera, a wide smile on her face.

I nodded. "It's yours. Keep it."

I had attended the prom with Trent Adams, of all people. Eli was grounded, but he thought I'd have fun with his friend at my side.

"We'll go together next year," he promised.

I wasn't going to go at all, but Trent suggested we dress up like we were from the 1920s, which sounded fun. I wore a silver flapper dress and decorated my hair with feathers. Trent wore a white tux and top hat and drew a thin mustache above his lip. We were a hit.

Prom was a success, despite the committee's worries that Tiffany's party would hurt attendance. Even Tiffany showed up, but all she did was comment on the girls' clothes. If a girl wore the same dress to prom that she'd worn to the party—and most of them did—Tiffany loudly pointed it out. Some of the seniors eventually asked her to leave. As she stormed out of the room there was a sprinkling of applause, but within a minute everyone had returned to dancing and chatting as if Tiffany had never even been there.

Once the camera crew left town and the party was a distant memory, Tiffany's reputation lost some of its luster. When word got out that she was going to be suspended for a racially insensitive remark, it hurt her image even more, which I thought was kind of strange because the same people who ignored the incident when it happened were now loudly condemning her. In the end, Mr. Werner's lawyer argued that she never finished saying whatever it was she was going to say and therefore it could have been anything. The suspension never happened, but Tiffany did have to write an essay on tolerance.

"This is great," Lan said, handing me another photograph.

It was a picture of a group of seniors just before they walked onstage to receive their diplomas. I was standing behind them with my camera, and the way the lights were set up made it look like they were almost glowing. I took a profile shot, and Eden used a digital copy for the final edition of the newspaper. She also declared that I was going to be on her staff next year. She had been freaking out because her best photographer graduated and she didn't have a replacement. I became the new photo editor before the bell rang on the last day of school.

Lan was still looking through the stack of photos when the doorbell rang.

"Come in!" I hollered. Eli and Brady walked into the den. Eli was carrying a banana latte for me. He kissed my cheek and handed me the drink.

"Thanks," I said, taking a cautious sip to make sure it wasn't too hot.

"You're addicted," said Eli, shaking his head with a smile.

"One a day isn't addicted."

Brady sat next to Lan and looked at the pictures with her. I turned on the TV, but put it on Mute.

"Half hour," I announced. I sat on the floor, my back against the sofa. Eli sat down next to me.

"You ready for this?"

"Ready for it to be over," I said, taking a deep drink.

The promos had been airing for two weeks. "This princess has planned the perfect party," a female announcer said dryly. There was a shot of Tiffany on her canopied bed, painting her toenails, followed by her trying on dresses in a boutique while her mother watched. "But will her fairy tale have a happy ending?"

"This is not what I want!" Tiffany screamed into her phone. The next scene showed her shrieking as her new convertible pulled into view and someone in the crowd asking, "What happened to it?"

I knew everyone from school would be watching the episode and I was thankful that at least I wouldn't have to face them the next day—school had been out for over a week. Even after I had been cleared of everything, people still looked at me differently. The general assumption seemed to be that my dad had pulled some strings to get me out of trouble. I knew I couldn't convince everyone of the truth, so I gave up trying. It was liberating, in a way. I began raising my hand more often in class and expressing my opinion. I figured that if people didn't like what I had to say, so what. I felt like I could handle anything.

Eli was officially ungrounded; however, he had to work mornings at Something's Brewing and afternoons at the school. I only saw him a few times a week, but we talked on the phone every night. I loved to lie in the dark, staring at the stars on my ceiling as I sank into the sound of his voice.

"Can I have this one?" Brady asked. He held up one of the pictures from prom of him and Lan.

"Absolutely," I said. I was pleased that people liked my pictures. I enjoyed taking them, and I felt like it was something I could really good at doing. Eli was using some shots I took of his artwork for his college portfolio.

Lan cleared her throat. "I almost hate to bring this up, but guess what I heard about Reva?"

Eli shifted uncomfortably. He didn't like hearing her name, but for me she was an unpleasant memory and nothing more.

"Her grandma enrolled her at that private academy across town, the one with the uniforms."

I laughed. "Are you telling me that she's going to have to wear a blazer and a plaid skirt every day of her senior year?"

"Yep. And they have a really strict code about makeup and jewelry, too."

Even Eli laughed. "Is it wrong to feel just a little sorry for her?"

A promo flashed across the screen and we watched it without turning on the sound. I felt my stomach tighten. I knew I would be a part of Tiffany's episode and I knew it wouldn't be good. I was hoping that they didn't focus too much on me, although Brady said he thought it would be funny if I stole the show.

Eli squeezed my hand. "It's going to be fine," he whispered.

I squeezed back. My most awful moment was about to be broadcast to the world but, sitting with Eli and Lan and Brady, it didn't feel quite so bad. It was amazing, I thought, how my worst moment had led to some of my best.

Lan picked up the remote. "It's time," she said. "This is kind of exciting, really. We get to see everyone we know."

The show's theme song began and the credits rolled across the screen. I leaned into Eli, who wrapped one arm around my shoulder.

The show opened with a shot in front of our school and panned over to show the gorillas painted on the wall. We cheered when we saw it. Before the scene changed, there was a split-second shot of Mr. Gildea leaving the building.

When I turned in my history paper to Mr. Gildea months earlier, I wasn't sure what to expect. Instead of writing a long essay, I compiled ten of my favorite pictures into a booklet and used the same caption for each one. "This is art," I wrote beneath the photos. One showed Bonnie at work, knitting a blue sweater. Another one featured my mom icing an elaborate cake. I also included photos of my friends doing the things they loved most.

I concluded with a shot of the gorillas. Beneath that picture, I wrote that art is what we create with feeling. "Anyone who puts genuine and honest thought into something is an artist," I wrote.

Mr. Gildea liked it. "Very unorthodox," he said as he flipped through the pages. "But you make a clear point. Good job." He gave me a B+ and recommended me for a summer photography course open to high school students at the community college.

Eli reached for my hand as the invitation ceremony flashed across the screen. Tiffany called out names through her bullhorn. Some people squealed excitedly while others shook their heads and walked away. I felt like I should be paying more attention to the show, but my mind kept going back to my pictures and the essay, which I planned on using in my own college portfolio. I was proud of my work. I felt like I had gone beyond the assignment to find an answer I had needed for a long time.

I wasn't defining art.

I was defining myself.

★ ★ ★ ★ ★

Acknowledgments

I could offer a thousand thanks to the following people
and it would not be enough, but I'll try anyway.

Thank you to Robert Lettrick,
"inventor" of the banana latte
and diligent reader of first drafts.

Thank you to Kristi Purnhagen,
who offered a critical eye and sound suggestions.

Thank you to all the strong and supportive women
in my life, including Barbara Bresock, Mary Ruth Bresock,
Abby Elliot, Barbara Lohrstorfer, Nancy McDaniel,
Sayrah Namaste, Maxine Purnhagen, Christine Sagan,
Jeanne Schaal, Janet Sekerak and Lillian Tupes.

Thank you to Diane Bishop,
my high school English teacher.

Thank you to the entire staff
at the Middle Tyger Library in Duncan, South Carolina.

Thank you to Henry and Quinn,
who inspired me to get serious about all this book stuff.

And finally, thank you to Joe,
who always saw me as a writer.

NEW YORK TIMES AND USA TODAY
BESTSELLING AUTHOR

P.C. CAST

"I WILL GO."

Rather than follow her family's restrictive rules, centaur Brighid
chose to set out on her own to make friends and form relationships
with humans as well as centaurs.

Now she's facing her toughest challenge yet. While helping guide home a
grieving human—Cuchulainn, her friend Elphame's brother—Brighid finds
herself beginning to care for him. An emotion forbidden by her clan.

To add to her troubles, the Great Goddess has awoken the power of the
Shaman within Brighid—the first centaur so blessed in ages. And just as she's
torn between taking up a power she never expected and a love she's afraid to
admit to, Brighid receives a vision of a tragedy that might destroy everyone
she's ever cared about....

Brighid's Quest

Book two in the Partholon series
available now wherever books are sold!

HARLEQUIN
TEEN

JULIE KAGAWA

The IRON KING

MEGHAN CHASE HAS A SECRET DESTINY— ONE SHE COULD NEVER HAVE IMAGINED....

Something has always felt slightly off in Meghan's life, ever since her father disappeared before her eyes when she was six. She has never quite fit in at school...or at home.

When a dark stranger begins watching her from afar and her prankster best friend becomes strangely protective of her, Meghan senses that everything she's known is about to change.

But she could never have guessed the truth—that she is the daughter of a mythical faery king and a pawn in a deadly war. Now Meghan will learn just how far she'll go to save someone she cares about, to stop a mysterious evil no faery creature dare face...and to find love with a young prince who might rather see her dead than let her touch his icy heart.

Look for Book One of the Iron Fey series
Available now wherever books are sold!

HARLEQUIN TEEN

HTJK21008TRR